THEODOR FONTANE, the outstanding German novelist of the nineteenth century, was born in 1819 in Neuruppin, a garrison town north-west of Berlin in the Prussian province of Brandenburg, a descendant of French Huguenots who had settled there. After desultory schooling he trained as a pharmacist and worked as a journeyman in various towns, but was more interested in writing verse and translating English authors (having learnt the language by reading it). In 1849 he took the risky decision to make his living as a writer, and in the following year published two volumes of ballads. He paid three visits to Britain; during the last, from 1855 to 1859, he lived in London (joined in mid-stay by his wife and family), working as a freelance journalist and press agent for the Prussian embassy. He wrote two books about London and English life and an account of a trip to Scotland, *Jenseit des Tweed* (*Beyond the Tweed*), and subsequently chronicled the life and history of Berlin's hinterland and Bismarck's military campaigns; he was a war correspondent during the Franco-Prussian War of 1870–71 (he was taken prisoner but released after two months). Throughout his life he wrote and translated poetry, and was especially fond of Scottish ballads. His first novel, *Vor dem Sturm* (*Before the Storm*), was published when he was fifty-eight, to be followed by sixteen further novels and novellas, of which *Effi Briest,** *Cécile* and *Unwiederbringlich* (*No Way Back*) besides *Irrungen, Wirrungen* (*On Tangled Paths*) have been published in translation in Angel Classics.

---

* Now in Penguin Classics.

PETER JAMES BOWMAN completed a PhD on Fontane at Cambridge University, where he worked as a supervisor in German to undergraduates before turning to writing and translating. He has published numerous articles on German literature and, most recently, *The Fortune Hunter: A German Prince in Regency England* (2010), a biography of the celebrated Prussian landscape architect and matrimonial adventurer Hermann von Pückler-Muskau. He lives in Ely, Cambridgeshire.

THEODOR FONTANE

On Tangled Paths

An Everyday Berlin Story

Translated from the German with an afterword by
PETER JAMES BOWMAN

ANGEL BOOKS
London

First published in 2010 by
Angel Books, 3 Kelross Road, London N5 2QS

www.angelclassics.com

1 3 5 7 9 10 8 6 4 2

A CIP catalogue record for this book is available from the British Library

ISBN: 978-0-946162-77-2

This book is printed on acid free paper conforming to the British Library
recommendations and to the full American standard

Typeset in 10½ on 12½ pt Monotype Ehrhardt by
Ray Perry, Woodstock, Oxon.
Printed and bound in Great Britain by MPG Biddles Ltd, King's Lynn

Contents

Acknowledgements

This translation of *Irrungen, Wirrungen* is based on the edition of the novel published by Wilhelm Goldmann Verlag, Munich in 1980; the subtitle used in the newspaper serialization that preceded first publication in book form has been added. I should like to thank my publisher, Antony Wood, for his extensive editorial input, Rudolf Muhs for checking the accuracy of the afterword, and Godela Weiss-Sussex for finding the ideal illustration for the front cover.

P. J. B.

AT THE POINT where the Kurfürstendamm intersects the Kurfürstenstrasse, diagonally across from the Zoological Gardens, there was still, in the mid-eighteen-seventies, a large market garden running back to the open fields behind; and in it stood a small, three-windowed house with its own little front garden, set back about a hundred paces from the road that went by and clearly visible from there despite being so small and secluded. However, the other building in the market garden, indeed without doubt its main feature, was concealed by this little house as if by the wings of a stage set, and only a red- and green-painted wooden turret with the remains of a clock face (no trace of an actual clock) under its pointed roof suggested that there was something hidden in the wings, a suggestion confirmed by a flock of pigeons fluttering up round the turret from time to time and, even more, by the occasional barking of a dog. The whereabouts of this dog eluded the viewer, although the front door on the far left stood open all day long, affording a glimpse of the yard. There was in general no apparent intention to hide anything, and yet anyone who passed that way at the time our story begins had to be content not to see beyond the little three-windowed house and a few fruit trees standing in the front garden.

It was the week after Whitsun, when the dazzling light of the long days sometimes seemed never-ending. But today the sun was already behind the Wilmersdorf church steeple, and the rays that had beaten down all day were now replaced by evening shadows in the front garden, its almost fairy-tale calm exceeded only by the calm of the little house, in which old Frau Nimptsch and her foster-daughter Lene lived as tenants. Frau Nimptsch herself was, as usual, sitting by the large but barely one-foot-high hearth in her front room which occupied the whole width of the house, and she crouched forward gazing at a sooty old kettle whose lid kept rattling even though steam was already billowing from the spout. The old woman stretched both hands out to the glowing embers and was so absorbed in her thoughts and daydreams that she did not hear the door out into the hallway opening and a sturdy female figure bustling into the room. It was only when the latter had cleared her throat and addressed her friend and neighbour (our Frau Nimptsch) warmly by name that she turned towards the back of the room and, just as amiably and with a touch of mischief, replied, 'Ah, Frau Dörr, my dear, how good of you to drop by, and from the "castle" too, 'cos it *is* a castle an' always will be, with its tower an' all. Now sit yourself down ... I just saw your dear husband goin' off somewhere. Course – it's his skittles night.'

The visitor so warmly greeted as Frau Dörr was not merely sturdy but of decidedly imposing proportions, and gave the impression of being a kind-hearted, dependable soul but also a person of distinctly limited intelligence. This clearly in no way troubled Frau Nimptsch, who repeated, 'Yes, his skittles night. But what I've been meanin' to say, my dear, is that your husband can't go about in that hat no more. It's worn smooth an' a proper disgrace to look at. You ought to take it off him and put a new one out. He mightn't even notice ... Now pull up a chair, Frau Dörr, my dear, or better, sit on that stool over there ... As you see, Lene's gone out an' left me on my own again.'

'So he was here, then?'

'Certainly was. An' they've gone out Wilmersdorf way.

You never meet no one on that path. But they should be back any minute.'

'Well, I'd best be goin', then.'

'No need, Frau Dörr, my dear. He won't stop. An' even if he does, he's not, you know, like *that*.'

'I know, I know. An' how do things stand?'

'Well, what can I say? I think she's gettin' ideas, even if she won't admit it, buildin' her hopes up.'

'Dear oh dear,' said Frau Dörr, as she drew up a slightly higher stool than the footstool she had been offered. 'Dear oh dear, that *is* bad. When they start gettin' ideas, that's when things turn bad. Sure as night follows day. You see, Frau Nimptsch, my dear, I was in the same boat, but I never got no ideas. And 'cos of that it was quite a different kettle of fish.'

She could see that Frau Nimptsch did not quite grasp her meaning, and so went on, 'It was 'cos I never got no ideas into my head that it all worked out so smooth an' easy, and now I've got Dörr. It's not much, I know, but it's respectable, and you can show your face anywhere. And that's why I went to church with him and not just the registry office. If you don't do it in church they'll always talk.'

Frau Nimptsch nodded, but Frau Dörr repeated, 'Yes, in church. St Matthew's it was and Büchsel* took the service. But you see, what I really meant to say, my dear, is that I was actually taller and more takin' than Lene, an' if I wasn't prettier ('cos you can't really know, and tastes do vary), well, there was a bit more of me, which there's some as like. No doubt about it. But even though I was fuller, you might say, with more substance, an' even though there was somethin' about me, p'raps – yes, there definitely was somethin' about me – still I was always quite straightforward, almost a bit simple. An' as for *him*, my count, fifty years old if he was a day, he really was

---

* Carl Albert Ludwig Büchsel (1803-89), prominent Lutheran clergyman known for his memoirs and published sermons.

a simple soul, always as cheery as can be an' indecent with
it. An' if I told him once I told him a hundred times: "No,
no, Count, *that* I won't have, I draw the line at *that* ..." And
that's how the old 'uns always are. I tell you, Frau Nimptsch,
my dear, you just can't imagine it. Dreadful it was. An' when
I look at Lene's baron I still feel right ashamed of what mine
was like. An' as for Lene, she's no angel, I don't suppose, but
she's a tidy, hard-workin' girl, can turn her hand to anythin',
an' with a sense of what's right and proper. An' you see, my
dear, that's the sad thing about it. The ones that gad about all
over the place, they fall on their feet and never come to grief,
but a good girl like her that takes it all to heart an' does it all
for love, *that's* bad ... Or maybe it isn't; after all you only took
her in, she's not your own flesh and blood, an' maybe she's a
princess or somethin'.'

Frau Nimptsch shook her head at this notion and seemed
about to answer. But Frau Dörr had already stood up and,
looking down the garden path, said, 'Lord, here they come.
And not even in uniform, jus' a plain coat an' trousers. But
you can tell just the same! An' now he's whisperin' in her
ear, and she's laughin' a bit to herself. Oh, she's gone all red
... And now he's leavin'. An' now I think ... yes, he's turnin'
round again. No, no, he's just givin' her another wave, and
she's blowin' him a kiss ... That's the way. Yes, that's what I
like to see ... No, not a bit like mine, not a bit.'

And Frau Dörr went on talking until Lene came in and
greeted them both.

2

THE FOLLOWING MORNING the sun, already quite high in
the sky, shone down on the yard of the Dörrs' market garden
and illuminated a whole cluster of buildings, among them

the 'castle' of which Frau Nimptsch had spoken the previous
evening with a trace of mockery and mischief. Yes, that
'castle'! At dusk its bulky silhouette really could make it pass
for something of the sort, but today, in the pitilessly bright
light, it could be seen only too clearly that the entire edifice,
painted up to the top with Gothic windows, was nothing more
than a wretched wooden box, into the two gable ends of which
a straw- and clay-filled timber framework had been inserted,
forming a comparatively solid structure that supported a
pair of attic rooms. The rest of the space had a simple stone
floor, and from it a tangle of ladders led first to a loft and then
higher up into the turret that served as a dovecote.

Earlier, in the pre-Dörrian period, the whole of this huge
wooden box had been used as a barn for storing beanpoles
and watering cans, and perhaps also as a potato cellar; but
from the time, umpteen years ago, when the market garden
was purchased by its present owner, the house itself was
let to Frau Nimptsch and the Gothic-painted box fitted up
by the addition of the aforementioned two attic rooms to
make a living space for Dörr, then a widower – a most primitive arrangement which his remarriage soon afterwards did
nothing to alter. In summer this almost windowless barn with
its flagstones and its coolness was not a bad place to live, but
in wintertime Dörr and his wife, together with a twenty-year-
old, slightly mentally deficient son from his first marriage,
would simply have frozen to death had it not been for the
two large hothouses on the other side of the yard. It was
exclusively in these that all three Dörrs spent November to
March; but in the more clement months too and even at the
height of summer – except when shelter was needed from the
sun – family life was carried on mainly in and around these
hothouses, because here everything lay most conveniently
to hand: here were the shelves and stands on which flowers
from the hothouses were placed each morning to freshen
in the open; here was a shed for the cow and the goat and a

kennel for the dog that pulled the cart; and from here a pair
of hotbeds, a good fifty paces long with a narrow path in
between, stretched to the large vegetable garden further to
the rear.

This vegetable garden was not exactly neat and tidy, partly
because Dörr was not given to order, but also because he
had such a strong passion for chickens that he allowed these
favourites of his to peck around everywhere without regard
to the damage they caused. Not that this damage was ever
great, for apart from the asparagus beds his market garden
contained nothing of the choicer sort. Dörr held that the
commonest things were also the most profitable, and therefore grew marjoram and oregano, but most of all leeks,
reflecting his abiding principle that the true Berliner requires
only three things: wheat beer, Gilka Kümmelschnapps and
leeks. 'With leeks,' he would regularly conclude, 'you always
get your money's worth.' He was altogether quite a character,
with a most independent outlook and a complete disregard
for what other people said about him. His second marriage
was of a piece with this, a marriage of inclination to which he
had been prompted in part by the notion of his wife's especial
beauty, her earlier relationship with the count, rather than
damaging her in his eyes, having on the contrary weighed
decisively in her favour by furnishing conclusive proof of her
irresistibility. And although this could fairly be described as
an overestimation, it was no such thing coming from someone
like Dörr, to whom nature had been exceptionally ungenerous
as far as outward appearance was concerned. A thin man of
medium height with five strands of grey hair across his head
and brow, he would have cut an utterly commonplace figure
had it not been for a brown pockmark between his left eye and
temple which made him look distinctive. And on this account

his wife was not wrong when she said from time to time, in her own uninhibited style, 'All shrivelled up he is, but from the left side he does look a bit like a Borsdorf apple.'[*]

The description captured him to a nicety and would have identified him to anyone but for the fact that day in, day out he wore a linen cap with a large peak pulled down so far over his face as to hide both the ordinary and the singular aspects of his physiognomy.

And thus he stood again the day after the conversation between Frau Dörr and Frau Nimptsch, his peaked cap pulled over his face, in front of a flower-stand supported against the first hothouse, setting aside various pots of wallflowers and geraniums that were to go to the weekly market the next day. All of these plants had simply been transferred to their pots rather than grown in them, and he lined them up before him with particular satisfaction and delight, already laughing in anticipation at the well-to-do housewives who would come along on the morrow, haggle their usual five pfennigs off the price, and still end up being gulled. This counted among his greatest pleasures and was the chief purpose to which he applied his intellect: 'That bit of cussin' ... wouldn't I love a chance to overhear it.'

He was just saying this to himself when from the direction of the garden he heard the barking of a little cur interspersed with the desperate crowing of a cock, unless he was quite mistaken *his* cock, his favourite of the silver plumage. And directing his gaze towards the garden he saw that a group of chickens had indeed been scattered, while the cock had flown up into a pear tree, from which he called uninterruptedly for help against the yapping dog below.

'Blast it!' cried Dörr furiously, 'that's Bollmann's again ... he's got through the fence again ... I know what I'll ...' And

---

[*] Originating in Borsdorf near Leipzig and often exhibiting small brown marks.

quickly putting down the potted geranium he was inspecting, he ran towards the kennel, grabbed the chain-clasp and released the large cart-dog, which shot straight over to the garden like a creature possessed. However, before he could reach the pear tree 'Bollmann's' took to its heels and vanished under the fence to the open ground beyond. At first the fox-coloured cart-dog bounded along behind, but the gap under the fence, just the right size for the affenpinscher, denied him exit and forced him to desist from his pursuit.

Just as unsuccessful was Dörr himself, who had meanwhile arrived on the scene with a rake and now exchanged looks with his dog. 'Well, Sultan, no luck this time.' At which Sultan made his way slowly back to his kennel, looking abashed as if he had detected a hint of reproach in this remark. For his part Dörr stared after the affenpinscher for a while as it raced along a furrow in the open field, and then said: 'I'll be damned if I don't get myself an air gun from Mehles' or somewhere. And then I'll quietly do away with the brute and no one'll give two hoots, leastways not my own hens and cock.'

For the moment the latter appeared to entertain no thought of observing the silence expected of him by Dörr, continuing instead to make the greatest possible use of his voice. And in doing so he proudly threw out his silver neck, as if to show the hens that his flight into the pear tree had been either a carefully considered ploy or a mere whim.

But Dörr said: 'There's a cock for you. Thinks the world of himself, but he's no big hero after all.'

And with that he walked back to his flower-stand.

3

ALL THIS had been observed by Frau Dörr, who was cutting asparagus, but she did not pay much attention because the same course of events was repeated nearly every other day. Instead she carried on working, and only when even the closest scrutiny of the beds revealed no more 'white-tips' did she give up her search. Then she hooked the basket over her arm, placed her knife inside it, and, driving a few stray chicks before her, walked slowly towards the central path through the garden and from there to the yard and the flower-stand, where Dörr had resumed his preparations for market day.

'Well, my little Susel,' he greeted his better half, 'so that's where you are. Did you see? That beast of Bollmann's was here again. He's got a nasty accident comin' his way, an' then I'll roast all the fat there is out of him, an' Sultan can have the crispy bits ... An' you know, Susie, dog fat ...' But just as he seemed about to dilate on the method of treating gout he had favoured for some time, he noticed the basket of asparagus on his wife's arm and checked himself. 'Now, give us a look, then. Any good?'

Frau Dörr held out the barely half-full basket to him. He shook his head as he ran its contents through his fingers, for it was mostly thin stalks with a lot of broken pieces mixed in.

'Listen, Susel, there's no denyin' it, you've got no eye for asparagus.'

'I have too, but I can't work miracles.'

'Well, let's not argue, Susel; that won't give us no more. But you could starve to death on that.'

'I don't think so. Leave off your talk for a change, Dörr. They're in the ground, aren't they, an' it makes no odds if they come out today or tomorrow. Just needs a nice heavy shower like before Whitsun, and then you'll see ... An' it'll rain all right. The water butt's started smellin' again and the big spider's crawled into the corner. But you want it all every day, and that's askin' too much.'

Dörr laughed. 'Well, tie it all up nice and tight, the scrubby bits too. You can always knock a bit off.'

'Don't talk like that,' his wife interrupted. She was forever getting irritated at his meanness, and she tweaked his earlobe in her customary way, which he always took as a sign of affection, and then made her way to the Castle, where she meant to make herself comfortable in the stone-floored area and tie up her asparagus bundles. But hardly had she moved the stool that always stood ready there out towards the doorway when she heard a rear window of Frau Nimptsch's little three-windowed house diagonally opposite being opened with a vigorous push and then put on the latch. At the same time she saw Lene, wearing a loose, lilac-patterned jacket over a frieze skirt and a little bonnet on her ash-blond hair, giving her a friendly wave.

Frau Dörr returned the greeting with equal warmth and then said, 'That's right, always open your windows wide, Lene, my poppet. It's gettin' hot already. It'll turn before the day's out, mind.'

'Yes, and mother's already got her headache from the heat, so I thought I'd rather do the ironing in the back room. It's nicer here anyway. You never see a soul at the front.'

'You're right,' answered Frau Dörr. 'Well, I'll just shift myself a bit closer to the window. Makes the work go quicker if you've got someone to talk to.'

'Oh, that really is kind of you, Frau Dörr. But here by the window you'll be right in the sun.'

'That won't harm, Lene. I'll fetch my market umbrella. It's an old thing, full of patches, but it still does the job.'

And not five minutes later the good Frau Dörr had dragged her stool over to the window and settled herself there under her standing umbrella, as comfortable and self-possessed as if she were on the Gendarmenmarkt.* Inside, meanwhile, Lene had placed her ironing board on two chairs moved up against

---

* Famous Berlin square commonly used for markets. Its name derives from the Gensdarmes cavalry regiment which deployed there in the previous century.

the window, and now stood so close to the other woman that they could easily have reached out and shaken hands. The iron went briskly back and forth, and Frau Dörr too was busy with her sorting and binding. Now and again she raised her eyes from her work, and through the window she saw the little stove that supplied freshly heated slugs for the iron glowing on the far side of the room.

'Could you just give me a plate, Lene, a plate or a bowl.' Lene promptly brought the desired article to Frau Dörr, who then filled it with the broken bits of asparagus she had put in her apron as she sorted through the stalks. 'There, Lene, that'll do for some asparagus soup. An' it's as good as the rest. People always want the tips, but that's daft. Same with cauliflower. The flower's what they want, always the flower, they can't get it out of their minds. But it's the stem that's the best bit. That's where the goodness is, an' it's the goodness that counts.'

'Lord, you're always so kind, Frau Dörr. But what will your old man say?'

'Him? Who cares what he says, my pet? It's all talk with him. He's always after me tyin' in the scrubby stuff as if it was the real thing, but I don't like that sort of trickery, even if the broken bits without tips do taste as good as the ones with everythin' on. You should get what you pay for, an' it makes me angry that someone like him that's doin' very nicely is such an old skinflint. But market gardeners are all the same, always graspin' for more an' never satisfied.'

'Yes,' Lene laughed, 'he is stingy and a bit odd in his ways. But still a good husband, I'm sure.'

'Yes, my pet, he wouldn't be too bad, an' even his stinginess I could live with – it's better than blowin' it all – if only he wasn't so affectionate. Never leaves me alone – you wouldn't believe it. An' just look at him. He really is a poor figure of a man, an' all of fifty-six too, or maybe more, 'cos he tells lies when it suits him. And there's no way I can stop him, no way at all. I keep tellin' him about people gettin' strokes an' I point them out, hobblin' along with crooked mouths, but he just laughs and won't believe it. It'll happen, mind. Yes, my pet, I'm quite sure it'll happen. Maybe quite soon. Still, everythin' comes to me in his will, so I'll say no more. As you make your bed, so you must lie on it. But what are we doing talkin' about strokes and Dörr with his bandy legs. Lord, there's a very different sort of man, as tall an' straight as a spruce tree, isn't there, Lene, my poppet?'

At this Lene grew even more flushed than she already was. 'This slug's gone cold,' she said, and stepped back from the ironing board and went over to the cast-iron stove to shake the slug out onto the coals and take up a new one. It was all the work of an instant. Then with a deft movement she slid the new red-hot slug from the end of the poker into the iron, shut its little panel back up, and only then observed that Frau Dörr was still waiting for an answer. To make sure, however, the good woman asked her question again and then added, 'Is he comin' today?'

'Yes, at least he said he would.'

'Tell me now, Lene,' continued Frau Dörr, 'how did it start? Mother Nimptsch never says nothin', an' if she does it's all vague, neither one thing nor another. Only tells half the story an' gets the whole thing mixed up. So you tell me. Is it true it was in Stralau?'

'Yes, Frau Dörr, it was in Stralau, Easter Monday, but already so warm it could have been Whitsun, and because Lina Gansauge wanted to go rowing we found ourselves a boat, and Rudolf – you probably know him, a brother of Lina's – well, he took the oars.'

'Rudolf. Lord, but he's only a boy.'

'I know. But he reckoned he knew what to do, and kept saying, "Sit still, girlies, yer rockin' de boat" – he's got such a terrible Berlin way of talking. But we were doing no such thing because we could see straight away that his boating skills weren't up to much. After a bit, though, we forgot to worry and just let ourselves drift along, bantering with people who passed by and splashed us. In one of the boats going in the same direction as ours there were a couple of very fine gentlemen who kept waving at us, and in our high spirits we waved back, and Lina even shook her hanky and acted as if she knew them, which she didn't; she was just showing off because she's still so young. And while we were laughing and joking and just toying with the oars, suddenly we saw the steamer coming at us from Treptow. As you can imagine, dear Frau Dörr, we had the shock of our lives, and in our terror we shouted to Rudolf to row us out of the way. But the boy lost his head and just rowed us round in circles. By now we were screaming and would certainly have been hit if the two men in the other boat hadn't immediately taken pity on us in our danger. With a couple of strokes they were along-side us, and while one of them pulled our boat firmly and quickly over with a hook and attached it to theirs, the other rowed us all clear of the swirling water – just for a moment it seemed that the big wave coming at us from the steamer might overturn us. The captain actually wagged his finger at us (which I noticed for all my terror), but then it was all over, and a minute later we'd got to Stralau, and the two who'd so kindly rescued us jumped ashore and gave us their hands like real gentlemen to help us get out. And so there we were standing on the landing-stage next to Tübbecke's feeling very sheepish, and Lina crying miserably, and only Rudolf, who's just a stubborn, loud-mouthed urchin and always against the military – only Rudolf had a pig-headed look on his face as if to say: what a stupid fuss, I could have rowed you out of it too.'

'Yes, that's what he is, a loud-mouthed urchin; I know him. But what about the two gen'l'men? That's the important thing.'

'Well, first they made sure we were all right, and then they sat down at the table next to ours and kept looking over at us. And at about seven, when it was starting to get dark and we were getting ready to go home, one of them came up to ask if we would allow him and his friend to escort us. In my high spirits I laughed and said that they'd rescued us and a rescuer mustn't be denied anything, but they might want to reconsider because we lived more or less at the other end of the world, so getting there was quite a trek. To which he obligingly said "All the better." By then the other one had come over ... Oh, Frau Dörr, it might not have been the right thing to do, speaking straight off in such a free way, but I'd taken a liking to one of them, and putting on airs and acting coy is something I've never been able to do. And so we walked the whole way, first along the Spree and then by the canal.'

'And Rudolf?'

'He walked behind, as if he didn't know us, but he made sure he saw everything that was going on. Which was only right, with Lina being only eighteen and still a good, innocent girl.'

'Do you think so?'

'I'm sure, Frau Dörr. You only have to look at her. You can see that sort of thing at a glance.'

'Yes, mostly. But not always. And so they brought you back home, then?'

'Yes, Frau Dörr.'

'And then what?'

'Then ... Well, you know what happened. He came the next day to ask after me. And since then he's often come, and I'm always glad when he does. Lord, it's a pleasure just to have something going on. It's often so lonely out here. And as you know, Frau Dörr, mother's got nothing against it and she always says, "There's no harm in it, my child. Before you know it old age has crept up on you."'

'Yes, yes,' said Frau Dörr, 'I've heard Frau Nimptsch sayin' things like that too. And she's quite right. At least, it depends how you look at it, an' livin' by the catechism's always better, an' you could say best of all. You can believe me there. But I well know that it's not always possible, and some folk jus' don't want to. An' if they don't want to, well, there's no forcin' them. They have to find their own way, and mostly they do, providin' they're honest an' decent an' stick to their word. An' of course, whatever happens you've got to put up with it – can't go complainin'. An' if you realize all that and keep remindin' yourself of it, well, you can't go far wrong. The only thing wrong is if you start gettin' ideas.'

'Oh, my dear Frau Dörr,' Lene said laughingly, 'what are you thinking of? Ideas indeed! I'm not getting any ideas. If I love someone then I love him. That's enough for me, and I want nothing else from him at all, nothing, nothing at all. Just my heart beating faster and counting the hours till he comes and then not being able to wait till he's here again – that's what makes me happy, that's enough for me.'

'Yes,' said Frau Dörr with a quiet smile, 'that's the way, that's how it should be. But is it really true he's called Botho?* Surely no one can have a name like that. I mean, it's not Christian.'

'Yes they can, Frau Dörr.' And Lene was preparing to confirm the existence of such names when Sultan began to bark, and at the same instant they clearly heard someone stepping into the hallway. Sure enough, the postman appeared and brought two orders for Dörr and a letter for Lene.

'Lord, Hahnke,' cried Frau Dörr to the man covered in great beads of sweat before her, 'it's drippin' off you. Is it really that hot? An' only half past nine. I can see it's not much fun being a postman.'

And the good woman made to go and fetch a glass of fresh milk, but Hahnke declined. 'Can't stop now, Frau Dörr.

---

* A pagan Germanic name (pronounced *Bawtaw*) of the sort that gained renewed currency in the wake of the Romantic movement.

Another time.' And with that he left.

Meanwhile Lene had unsealed her letter.

'Well, what does he say?'

'He's not coming today, but he will tomorrow. Oh, it's so long till tomorrow. Good thing I've got work to do; the more work the better. And this afternoon I'll come over to your garden and help with the digging – but Dörr mustn't be there.'

'God forbid.'

And then they separated, and Lene went into the front room to take her old mother the portion of asparagus that Frau Dörr had given her.

4

IT WAS now the following evening and Baron Botho due to arrive. Lene paced up and down the front garden, while indoors Frau Nimptsch sat as usual in the big front room before the hearth, around which, as so often, the full complement of the Dörr family was also assembled. With big wooden needles Frau Dörr was knitting her husband a blue woollen cardigan, which, shapeless as yet, lay like a large fleece on her lap. Beside her was Dörr, his legs comfortably crossed, smoking a clay pipe, while his son sat in a big grandfather chair close by the window and leant his ginger-topped head against its wing; he was out of bed every morning at cockcrow, and would often, as now, be overcome by sleep in the evening. Nobody said much, and all that could be heard was the clicking of the wooden needles and the nibbling of the squirrel which came out of its little sentry-box from time to time and peered curiously around. The only light came from the fire in the hearth and the glow of the setting sun.

From where she sat Frau Dörr could see right up the

narrow garden path and, even in the twilight, make out anyone walking along the border hedge towards them.

'Ah, here he comes,' she said. 'Now Dörr, put that pipe out. You've been like a chimney again today, puffin' an' smokin' from mornin' till night. And the smell it belches out isn't to everyone's taste.'

Dörr paid little heed to these observations, and before his wife could enlarge on them or say anything else the baron walked in. He was visibly on the merry side, having come straight from imbibing a May punch, the object of a wager at his club, and he held out his hand to Frau Nimptsch and said, 'Good day to you, mother. Keeping well, I trust. And Frau Dörr as well, and Herr Dörr, my old friend and benefactor. I say, Dörr, what do you think of the weather? Just the thing for you, and for me too. My meadows at home, which are under water four years in five and produce nothing but buttercups – they can do with weather like this. It'll do Lene good too, get her out of the house more; she's been getting a trifle pale for my liking.'

As he spoke Lene placed a wooden chair next to the old woman, knowing that this was where Baron Botho best liked to sit; but by this time Frau Dörr, who was strongly of the view that a baron must sit in the place of honour, had stood up and, trailing her blue fleece behind her, shouted to her stepson, 'Come on, get up! Honestly! But what do you expect when he's got nothin' between his ears?' Still befuddled by sleep, the poor boy shot to his feet and made to give up his seat, but the baron would not hear of it: 'For heaven's sake, my dear Frau Dörr, let the boy alone. I'd far rather sit on a stool like my friend Dörr here.'

And with that he pushed the wooden chair that Lene was still holding ready next to the old woman, and as he sat down he said, 'Here next to Frau Nimptsch, that's the best place. I can think of no other hearth I'd rather gaze at. Always a fire in it and plenty of warmth. Yes, mother, it's the truth: this is the best place of all.'

'Well, goodness me,' said the old woman. 'This the best place, at an old ironing-and-washerwoman's house!'

'Of course. And why not? Each station in life has its dignity, including a washerwoman's. Did you know, mother, that a famous poet once lived here in Berlin who wrote a poem about his old washerwoman?'[*]

'It's not possible.'

'Of course it's possible. In fact it's certain. And do you know what he said at the end of it? He said he'd like to live and die like the old washerwoman. Yes, that's what he said.'

'It's not possible,' muttered the old woman again with a quiver in her voice.

'And you know, mother, there's something else too: he was quite right and I say exactly the same thing myself. You're laughing to yourself, but look around and see how you live. Like God in France.[†] For a start you've got this house and its hearth, and then the garden and then Frau Dörr. And then you've got Lene. Isn't that so? But where on earth is she?'

He would have carried on, but at that instant Lene returned with a coffee tray bearing a carafe of water along with some cider – this odd preference of the baron's being due to his belief in its extraordinary curative powers.

'Oh, Lene, how you spoil me! But you mustn't serve it to me in such a formal way; it's just as if I were at the Club. You should hand it to me – then it'll taste best. And now give me your little paw so that I can stroke it. No, no, the left one, nearest your heart. And now sit down here, between Herr and Frau Dörr, so that you're facing me and I can have a good look at you. I've been looking forward to this moment all day.'

---

[*] In Adelbert von Chamisso's 'Die alte Waschfrau' ('The Old Washerwoman') of 1833 the poet admires the washerwoman's dutiful devotion to work, which gives her life a sense of fulfilment his lacks.

[†] A set phrase in German.

Lene laughed.

'You don't believe me, do you? But I can prove it to you, Lene, because I've brought you a little present from the great occasion we had yesterday – the Patronesses' Ball. And when you've brought a present you look forward to seeing the people you want to give it to. Isn't that right, my dear Dörr?'

Dörr grinned, but Frau Dörr said, 'Lord, *him* bring a present! All he thinks of is scrimpin' and savin'. That's market gardeners for you. But I'm curious to see what the Herr Baron has brought along.'

'Well, in that case I won't keep you waiting any longer, my dear Frau Dörr, otherwise you'll start thinking it's a golden slipper or something else from a fairy tale. It's just *this*.'

And he handed Lene a paper bag with what looked very much like the fringed ends of some party crackers peeping out of the top.

They were indeed crackers, and the bag was passed round.

'And now we must pull one, Lene. Hold tight and close your eyes.'

Frau Dörr was delighted by the bang, and even more so when Lene's forefinger began to bleed. 'That doesn't hurt, Lene, I know about that; it's like a bride prickin' her finger. I knew one once that was so struck on the idea that she kept on prickin' and then sucked and sucked as if a miracle might happen.'

Lene reddened, but Frau Dörr did not notice and went on, 'And now, Herr Baron, read the motto out to us.'

And he read:

'To see us lose ourselves in love
Gives joy to the Lord and his angels above.'

'Lord,' said Frau Dörr, folding her hands, 'Jus' like out of the hymn book. Are they all so religious?'

'No, no,' said Botho. 'Not always. Come on, my dear Frau

Dörr, you pull one with me, and we'll see what we get.'

And so he pulled another one and read:

> 'When Cupid aims his dart too well
> He opens the gates of heaven and hell.'

'Now, Frau Dörr, what do you say to that? That's got a different ring to it, hasn't it?'

'Well,' said Frau Dörr, 'it certainly has, but I'm not sure as I like it ... When I pull a cracker ...'

'Yes?'

'There shouldn't be anythin' about hell in it. I don't want to hear that there is such a place.'

'Nor do I,' said Lene with a laugh. 'Frau Dörr's quite right; in fact she's always right. All the same, it's true that if you read out a motto like that it does give you something to start with, start a conversation, I mean, because starting's always the hardest part, just like when you're writing a letter, and I really can't imagine how you manage to break the ice and get a conversation going with so many ladies you don't know – and you can't be acquainted with all of them.'

'Ah, my dear Lene,' said Botho, 'it's not as hard as you think. In fact it's quite easy. If you like I'll make up a dinner-table conversation for you now.'

Frau Dörr and Frau Nimptsch expressed delight at the idea, and Lene too nodded in agreement.

'Well,' continued Baron Botho, 'imagine you're a young countess, and I've just escorted you to the table and sat down and now we're taking our first spoonful of soup.'

'Yes, yes. And then?'

'And then I say, "Unless I'm mistaken, my gracious Countess, I saw you yesterday at the Flora, you and your Mama. And who can blame you? With the weather so fine one's tempted out of doors every day, and it's already quite like holiday weather. Have you made any plans, my gracious

Countess, plans for the summer?" And now you answer that unfortunately nothing is fixed yet because your Papa is intent on the Bavarian Alps, whereas you have set your heart on Saxon Switzerland with its Königstein and its Bastei.'

'I really have too,' laughed Lene.

'You see, it all fits together. And so then I go on, "Well, my gracious Countess, our tastes entirely coincide on that point. I prefer Saxon Switzerland to any other part of the world, even the real Switzerland. One can't always be swooning over the grandeur of nature, or climbing and getting out of breath. But Saxon Switzerland! Heavenly, perfect! Then there's Dresden nearby, less than half an hour away, with its pictures, its theatres, the Grosser Garten, the Zwinger, the Grünes Gewölbe Collection. Don't forget to have someone show you the Pitcher with the Foolish Virgins, and above all the cherry stone with the entire Lord's Prayer on it. Only visible through a magnifying glass."'

'So that's how you talk!'

'Just like that, my darling. And when I've finished speaking to my neighbour on the left, with Countess Lene that is, I turn to my neighbour on the right, that is to Baroness Dörr ...'

In her delight Frau Dörr struck her hand on her knee with a loud thump ...

'To Baroness Dörr then. But what should I talk about? I know – sponge mushrooms.'

'Dear Lord, sponge mushrooms! But you can't, Herr Baron, not about sponge mushrooms.'

'Why ever not, why not talk about that, my dear Frau Dörr? It's a very serious and instructive topic, and it means more to some people than you might realize. I once visited a friend in Poland – we'd fought in the same regiment – who lived in a big red castle with two fat towers and so frightfully old you never saw one like it. And the furthest room was his living room; he wasn't married, you see, because he was a misogynist ...'

'Well I never!'

'And everywhere there were rotten floorboards, all trodden through, and wherever a few floorboards were missing there was a bed of these sponge mushrooms, and I had to walk past all these beds until at last I reached his room.'

'Well I never!' repeated Frau Dörr, and then added, 'Sponge mushrooms. But you can't always be talking about sponge mushrooms.'

'No, not always. But often, or at least sometimes, and to be honest it makes no difference what you talk about. If not sponge mushrooms then ordinary mushrooms, and if not the red castle in Poland then the Tegel Palace, or Saatwinkel, or Valentinswerder. Or Italy or Paris, or the metropolitan railways, or whether the River Panke ought to be filled in. It makes no difference at all. You can say something about anything, and whether you like it or not. And a "yes" is as good as a "no".'

'But,' said Lene, 'I'm surprised you go to entertainments like that if it's all just empty talk.'

'Oh, but you see beautiful women in fine dresses, and if you pay attention you sometimes catch a glance that tells you a whole hidden story. In any case, it never goes on too long, there's always time to catch up at the Club. And the Club really is something; that's where the empty talk stops and reality starts. Yesterday I took Pitt's black Graditz mare off him.'

'Who's Pitt?'

'Oh, those are just nicknames we use when we're among ourselves. Like the Crown Prince saying Vicky when he means Victoria. It's really good to have these pet names and terms of affection. But listen, the band's just starting over the way. Couldn't we open the windows so that we can hear it better? You're already jigging your foot. Why don't we take to the floor and try a contredanse or a quadrille? We'll make three pairs: Herr Dörr and my good Frau Nimptsch, and then Frau Dörr and myself (if I may have the honour), and then Lene and Hans.'

Frau Dörr agreed at once, but Frau Nimptsch and Dörr declined, the former because she was too old, the latter because he knew nothing of such fine things.

'Very well, old boy. But in that case you must beat time. Lene, give him the coffee tray and a spoon. Now step up, ladies. Frau Dörr, your arm. And Hans, wake up there, come on, come on.'

Both couples took their places, and Frau Dörr swelled to even more imposing proportions at her partner's direction *En avant deux, pas de basque*, delivered in his ceremonious dancing master's French. The freckled, unfortunately still half-asleep gardener's boy found himself being jerked mechanically around like a puppet, but the other three danced like real adepts, so captivating old Dörr that he got up from his stool and drummed the coffee tray with his knuckle instead of the spoon. Old Frau Nimptsch too felt the enthusiasm of former times returning, and, with nothing better to do, stirred the glowing coals round and round with the poker until the flames shot upwards.

So they went on until the distant music fell silent. Then Botho led Frau Dörr back to her seat, and only Lene remained standing because the clumsy gardener's boy did not know what to do with her. Which suited Botho perfectly, for when the music started up again he began waltzing with her and whispered in her ear how lovely she was, lovelier than ever.

They had all got warm, especially Frau Dörr, who now cooled herself at the open window. 'Lord,' she said suddenly, 'I'm all shiverin',' whereupon Botho obligingly sprang up to shut the window. But Frau Dörr would not hear of it, asserting that 'fine folk' were all in favour of fresh air, and some of them took it so far that in winter their bedding froze against their mouths, for breath was just like steam coming

out of the spout of a kettle. So the windows were to stay
open, she wouldn't budge on that. But if her little Lene had
something to warm her insides, something to cheer the heart
and soul ...

'Certainly, my dear Frau Dörr, whatever you like. I can
make some tea or punch, or, even better, I've still got the
kirsch you gave mother and me last Christmas to go with the
big almond fruitcake ...'

And before Frau Dörr could decide between tea and punch
the bottle of kirsch had arrived, with glasses large and small
into which they all poured out the measure they wanted.
Then Lene went round with the sooty kettle and added
boiling hot water. 'Not too much, Lene, my pet, not too
much. Always nice and strong. Water takes the goodness
away.' And in no time at all the room was filled with the
almond aroma of kirsch.

'Ah, you've done well there,' said Botho as he sipped from
his glass. 'Heaven knows, I had nothing as delicious as this
yesterday, let alone today at the Club. Long live Lene! But
the real credit goes to our friend Frau Dörr, because she was
"all shivering", and so now I'd like to propose a second toast:
Long live Frau Dörr!'

'Hear, hear!' came the mingled cries of the others, and
once again old Dörr drummed his knuckle on the tray.

They all agreed that it was a fine drink, much finer than
essence of punch, which in the summer always had a sour
lemon taste because it came from old bottles that had been
standing in the shop windows in the hot sunlight since
Shrovetide. But kirsch, that was good for you and never went
off, and although bitter almonds were poisonous you couldn't
harm yourself unless you drank an awful lot, at least a bottle.

This last remark was made by Frau Dörr, and her old
man, not wishing to see its accuracy put to the test, perhaps
because he well knew that his wife's ruling passion lay in this
direction, now sought to break up the party: tomorrow was

another day after all, he said.

Botho and Lene tried to persuade him to stay, but the good Frau Dörr, who knew that to retain the upper hand she must give way once in a while, said, 'Leave it, my pet, I know his ways; when the chickens go to bed so does he.'

'Well,' said Botho, 'that's that, then. But in that case we'll see the Dörr family to their door.'

And so they all set out, leaving only old Frau Nimptsch behind. She looked after them benignly and nodded her head, and then got up and went to sit in the grandfather chair.

5

BOTHO AND LENE stopped in front of the Castle with its red-and green-painted turret and asked Dörr with all ceremony if, as it was such a lovely evening, he would permit them to go for a half-hour stroll in the market garden. Dörr mumbled that he couldn't leave his property in better hands, whereupon the young couple bowed courteously, took their leave, and walked towards the garden. By now all was quiet except for Sultan, who drew himself up as they passed and whimpered until Lene stroked him. Only then did he creep back into his kennel.

Everything was fresh and fragrant in the garden, for the main path, which separated the currant from the gooseberry bushes, was bordered with stock and mignonette, whose delicate scent mingled with the stronger aroma coming from the thyme beds. Nothing stirred in the trees, and only fireflies darted through the air.

Lene had slipped her arm through Botho's, and together they walked to the end of the garden, where a bench stood between two white poplars.

'Shall we sit down?'

'No,' said Lene, 'not yet', and she turned into a side-path, where tall raspberry bushes almost reached over the top of the garden fence. 'I like walking on your arm so much. Tell me a story. But something really nice. Or ask me something.'

'All right. Do you mind if I begin with the Dörrs?'

'As you like.'

'A curious couple. But a happy one, I'd say. He has to do her bidding, and yet he's much the cleverer.'

'Yes,' said Lene, 'he is cleverer, but he's also stingy and hard-hearted, and that makes him submissive because he's forever got a bad conscience. She keeps a sharp eye on him and won't tolerate him trying to cheat anyone. And that's what he's afraid of and what keeps him under her thumb.'

'And nothing else?'

'Maybe love as well, odd though it sounds. Love on his part, I mean. Because although he's fifty-six, if not more, he's still besotted with his wife, just because of her size. They've both made the strangest confessions to me on that score. I don't mind admitting that she wouldn't be my taste.'

'I must say you're mistaken there, Lene; she cuts quite a figure.'

'Yes,' said Lene with a laugh, 'she might *cut* one, but she hasn't *got* one. Haven't you noticed that her hips are a hand's breadth too high? But you men don't notice things like that, you go on about "imposing" and "cutting a figure" without anyone caring what the imposingness is actually made up of.'

As they chatted and teased each other, Lene came to a stop, bent down by a long, narrow strawberry bed running along the fence and hedge, and looked for an early strawberry. At last she found what she wanted, placed the stem of a perfect specimen between her lips, and then stepped in front of him and looked at him.

Without hesitating he plucked the fruit from her mouth and then embraced her and kissed her.

'My sweet Lene, how beautifully you did that! But just

listen to Sultan barking; he wants to be with you. Shall I untie him?'

'No, if he's over here I'll only have you half to myself. And if you carry on about the imposing Frau Dörr I might as well not have you at all.'

'All right,' Botho laughed, 'Sultan can stay where he is. That's fine by me. But I'd like to talk a bit more about Frau Dörr. Does she really mean so well?'

'Yes, she does, although she says odd things, things that sound a bit like double-entendres and maybe are. But it's not intentional, and there's absolutely nothing in her behaviour that recalls her past.'

'Has she got one, then?'

'Yes. At least she had an affair for many years and "went with him", as she puts it. And there's no doubt that there's been gossip – a lot of gossip – about this affair and of course about the good Frau Dörr herself. And she'll have given the tongues plenty to wag about. Only she's such a simple soul that she's never given it a thought, let alone reproached herself. She speaks of it as a disagreeable service that she carried out faithfully and honestly out of a pure sense of obligation. You may laugh, and it does sound fairly odd, but there's no other way of describing it. And now let's stop talking about Frau Dörr and sit down and look at the crescent moon instead.'

There it was, standing above the Elephant House a little way off, and in its silver rays the building looked even more fantastical than usual. Lene pointed it out, pulled the hood of her cape closer around her head, and nestled against his chest.

A few minutes passed by in silent happiness, and then she roused herself as if from a dream she could not quite pin down, and said, 'What were you thinking? But you have to tell me the truth.'

'What was I thinking, Lene. Well, I'm almost ashamed to say. Sentimental things. I was thinking about our kitchen garden at home at Zehden Manor, which looks just like the Dörrs' here, the same lettuce beds with cherry trees in between, and I'll bet just as many tit-boxes. And asparagus beds laid out in the same way too. And I'd walk between them with my mother, and if she was in a good mood she'd give me the knife and let me assist her. But heaven help me if I was clumsy and cut the asparagus stalks too long or too short. My mother was quick with her hand.'

'I can believe it. I always feel I'd be afraid of her.'

'Afraid? Why? What do you mean, Lene?'

Lene laughed heartily, but there was a trace of constraint in her voice. 'You needn't think I'm intending to have myself introduced to her ladyship, and you mustn't take it any other way than if I'd said I was afraid of the Empress. Would you then think I wanted to be presented at court? No, don't be alarmed; I won't go and lodge any complaints against you.'

'No, I know you won't. You're far too proud for that, and you're a proper little democrat and have to squeeze your soul for every kind word you say to me. Am I right? Well, however it is, see if you can picture my mother in your mind. What does she look like?'

'Just like you: tall and slim and blond and blue-eyed.'

Now it was his turn to laugh. 'Poor Lene, you're a long way off the mark there. My mother's a small woman with lively black eyes and a large nose.'

'I don't believe it. It's not possible.'

'Oh yes it is. You must remember that I also have a father. But women never think of that. You always think you're the important thing. And now tell me something about my mother's character. But make a better guess this time.'

'I think of her as being very concerned about her children's welfare.'

'Now you've hit the mark –'

'– and that they should all make good matches, very good ones. And I also know who she's got lined up for you.'

'Some unfortunate girl that you –'

'How you misjudge me! Believe me, having you here now, having this time with you, that's my happiness. I don't worry about what the future holds. One day I'll find you've flown away …'

He shook his head.

'Don't shake your head; it's true, what I say. You love me and you're true to me – at least my love makes me childish and vain enough to imagine it. But fly away you will, I can see that very clearly. You'll have to. They always say love blinds, but it also opens our eyes and makes us far-sighted.'

'Oh, Lene, you've no idea how much you mean to me.'

'Yes, I do know. And I also know that you feel your Lene is someone special, and that every day you think: if only she were a countess. But it's too late for that now; it's beyond my powers. You love me but you're weak-willed. We can't change that. All handsome men are weak-willed, and ruled by a stronger force … And that stronger force … What is it? Well, either it's your mother or people's talk or circumstances. Or maybe all three … But look!'

And she pointed over to the Zoological Gardens, where a hissing rocket had just shot up from the black foliage of the trees into the air and now scattered with a clap into count-less firecrackers. The first was followed by a second, and so on, as if they were trying to chase and overtake one another, until suddenly it was all over, and the thickets in the area began to glow green and red. A few birds in their cages were screeching, and then, after a long interval, the music struck up again.

'You know, Botho, if I could take you to the Lästerallee[*] over there and walk up and down with you as confidently as I can here between these box hedges, and say to everyone:

---

[*] 'Slander Avenue', a walk through the Zoological Gardens lined with seats from which gossips would comment on passers-by.

"Yes, stare all you like, he's who he is and I'm who I am, and he loves me and I love him" – oh, Botho, what do you think I'd give for that? But don't try to guess, you wouldn't be able to. You and your friends only know your own circle and your Club and your life. Poor little scrap of life.'

'Don't talk like that, Lene.'

'Why not? You have to look facts honestly in the face and not let yourself be fooled, and especially not fool yourself. But it's getting cold, and it's all finished over there. That's the finale they're playing now. Come on, let's go and sit indoors by the hearth; the embers will still be burning, and mother will have gone to bed long ago.'

And so they made their way back up the garden path, she leaning lightly against his shoulder. By now the lights were all out in the Castle, and only Sultan, his head stretched out of his kennel, gazed after them. He did not stir this time, but kept his glum thoughts to himself.

6

It was the following week and the chestnut blossom had already faded, not least in the Bellevuestrasse, where Baron Botho von Rienäcker had a ground-floor apartment with balconies overlooking the front and the garden, and a study, dining room and bedroom, each decorated with conspicuous good taste and at an expense considerably beyond his means. In the dining room there were two Hertel still lifes and between them a valuable imitation of a Rubens *Bear Hunt*, while the study boasted a *Storm at Sea* by Andreas Achenbach, surrounded by a number of smaller works by the same master. The *Storm at Sea* he had acquired by winning it in a lottery, and this beautiful and costly possession had formed his eye as a connoisseur and in particular as an admirer of Achenbach. He liked to joke about this, declaring that by continually enticing him into further purchases his good fortune in the lottery had cost him dear, adding that the same was perhaps true of any piece of good fortune.

In front of the sofa, which had a Persian rug draped over its plush upholstery, was a small malachite table bearing the coffee things, while strewn on the sofa itself were assorted newspapers, some whose presence here would have surprised anyone who did not know the baron's pet saying that tittle-tattle comes before politics. Stories that bore the stamp of invention on their brow, the so-called 'pearls', amused him most. As usual the canary, whose cage always stood open at breakfast-time, flew over and perched on the hand and shoulder of its all too indulgent master, who, instead of being irritated, would always lay his newspaper aside and stroke his little favourite. If he omitted to do so the tiny creature would bore itself into his neck and beard as he read and chirp stubbornly until it got its way. 'All favourites are alike,' Baron Rienäcker liked to say, 'in demanding obedience and submission.'

Just then the corridor bell rang and the manservant came in with the letters that had been delivered at the door. One of these, in a square grey envelope, was unsealed and bore a three-pfennig stamp. 'A Hamburg lottery ticket or a new cigar promotion,' said Rienäcker, tossing the envelope and its contents aside without further investigation. 'But this one ... ah, from Lene. Well, *this* I'll save till last, unless this third sealed one claims priority. The Osten coat of arms, in other words from Uncle Kurt Anton; Berlin postmark, which means he's already here. Whatever can he want? Ten to one I'm to have lunch or buy a saddle with him or accompany him to Renz's, and maybe to the Kroll Gardens too – if not the whole lot together.'

And with a little knife lying on the windowsill he slit open the envelope, on which he had now also recognized Uncle

Kurt Anton's handwriting, and took out the letter.

Hotel Brandenburg, Room 15

My dear Botho,
I arrived safe and sound an hour ago at the Eastern Station,
where I was greeted by your old Berlin motto 'Beware of
Pickpockets', and have established myself at the Hotel
Brandenburg, in other words my usual quarters – it's
consistency in little things that makes the true conservative. I'm only staying two days as your Berlin air oppresses
me. What a muggy hole it is! More when we meet. I'll
expect you at Hiller's at one. Then we'll go and buy a
saddle. And then Renz's in the evening. Don't be late.

Your old Uncle Kurt Anton

Rienäcker laughed. 'I thought as much! One innovation
though. Before it was Borchardt's, now it's Hiller's. Tut, tut,
Uncle, what was that about little things and true conserva-
tives ...? And now for my darling Lene ... I wonder what
Uncle Kurt Anton would say if he knew what company his
letter and instructions are keeping.'

And as he spoke he opened Lene's note and read:

It's now five whole days since I last saw you. Will it be
a whole week? And I was so happy that evening that I
thought you were sure to come again the next day. You
were so dear and kind. Mother's already teazing me, saying
'He won't come any more'. Oh, it always cuts me to the
quick, because I know that it must end like that and I feel
it could happen any day. Yesterday I was reminded of it
again, because what I wrote just now about not seeing you
for five days isn't really true. I *have* seen you, yesterday
at the Korso,[*] in secret, without anyone knowing. Just

---

[*] The Blumenkorso, a procession featuring flower-bedecked carriages.

think, I was there too, a long way back of course in a side avenue, watching you ride up and down for an hour. Oh how thrilled I was, because you were more imposing than all the others (almost as imposing as Frau Dörr, who sends her greetings), and I was so proud at the sight of you that I didn't even feel jealous! Except for once, that is. Who was the beautiful blonde girl with the two white horses all covered with a big garlend of flowers? Such a mass of flowers, no leaves or stawks at all. I've never seen anything so beautiful in all my life. As a little girl I'd have thought she must be a princess, but now I know that princesses aren't always the best-looking. Yes, she really was beautiful, and I could see you took a fancy to her, and she did to you too. And as for her mother, who was sitting next to the beautiful blonde girl, *she* liked you even more. And that did prevoke me. I wouldn't begrudge you a very young one, if it really had to be, but an old one! And a mother too! No, no, she's had *her* share. Anyway, my own precious Botho, you can see that you'll have to sooth me and cheer me up. I'll be waiting for you tomorrow or the day after. And if you can't come in the evening, come during the day, even if it's only for a minute. I'm so afraid for you, or for myself I should say. You know what I mean.

Your Lene

He repeated the words 'Your Lene' at the end of the letter softly to himself, and an unease took hold of him caused by the sharply conflicting feelings – love, anxiety, fear – that filled his heart. Then he read the letter through once more. In two or three places he could not resist making a little mark with his silver pencil, not out of pedantry but in sheer delight. 'How well she writes! Her handwriting's excellent and her spelling's not bad at all. 'Garlend' instead of 'garland' ... Well, why not? Garland was a much-feared inspector of schools, but I'm not, thank God! And 'sooth'. Should I be

cross with her for missing an 'e' off the end? Heavens, how
many people can spell 'soothe' right? Young countesses not
always and old ones never. So where's the harm? The letter's
exactly like Lene herself – kind, faithful and dependable, and
the errors just give it an added charm.'

He leant back in his chair and covered his brow and eyes
with his hand. 'Poor Lene, what's to become of us? It would
have been better for us both if there hadn't been an Easter
Monday this year. Why are there two days of holiday anyway?
Why Treptow and Stralau and boating trips? And now here's
Uncle! Either he's come as my mother's envoy again, or
else he's got plans of his own for me, on his own initiative.
Well, I'll soon see. He hasn't had any training in diplomatic
dissimulation, and even if he's sworn a dozen oaths to keep
quiet it'll still slip out. I'll get it out of him, even though I'm
not much better at the art of intrigue than he is.'

As he pondered he opened a drawer of his bureau
containing other letters from Lene, all tied up with a red
ribbon. Then he rang for his manservant to come and help
him dress. 'Right, Johann, all done ... Now don't forget to
lower the blinds. And if anyone comes and asks for me I'm at
the barracks till twelve, at Hiller's from one and at Renz's in
the evening. And see that you pull the blinds back up again at
the right time – I don't want to come back and find the place
like a furnace again. And leave the front lamp burning. But
not in my bedroom; there's a real plague of mosquitoes this
year. Understood?'

'Very good, Herr Baron.'

This conversation was still going on as Rienäcker walked
through the corridor and into the entrance hall of the building.
Outside in the front garden he gave the thirteen-year-old
porter's daughter's plait a tug from behind as she leant over
her little brother's pram, to be met by a furious face which
melted instantly into tenderness when she saw who it was.

Then he went through the iron gate into the street. Here

he looked beneath the green chestnut foliage towards the Brandenburg Gate and then towards the Tiergarten, where people and carriages were moving noiselessly back and forth like images focused on a camera obscura screen. 'How beautiful! This really is one of the best of all possible worlds.'

7

AT MIDDAY barrack duty was over, and Botho von Rienäcker made his way along Unter den Linden towards the Brandenburg Gate. His aim was simply to fill the hour before his appointment at Hiller's as best he could, and he was therefore very glad of the two or three art dealers' shops that lay on his path. At Lepke's there were a few Oswald Achenbachs in the window, among them a street scene in Palermo, dirty and sunny, remarkably authentic as a study of life and colour. 'There really are some things it's impossible to make up one's mind about. These Achenbachs, for example. Until recently I'd have sworn by Andreas, but when I see something like this here I'm not at all sure that Oswald doesn't equal or even surpass him. He's certainly got more colour and variety. But I'd better keep such thoughts to myself, because if I start telling other people I'll quite needlessly halve the value of my *Storm at Sea*.'

He stood for a while at Lepke's window turning all this over in his mind, then walked across the Pariser Platz towards the Gate and the Tiergartenallee forking off to the left, stopping in front of Wolf's bronze lions. He checked his watch. 'Half past twelve. It's time.' He turned round to take the same way back to Unter den Linden. In front of the Palais Redern he saw Lieutenant von Wedell of the Dragoon Guards coming his way.

'Where are you off to, Wedell?'

'The Club. And you?'

'Hiller's.'

'Rather early.'

'Yes, but can't be helped. I'm lunching with an old uncle of mine, a true sprig of the Neumark from the Bentsch-Rentsch-Stentsch neck of the woods – all places that rhyme with *Mensch*, though they don't let that bother them. In fact he once served in your regiment – my uncle, I mean. Long while back, of course, early forties. Baron Osten.'

'From Wietzendorf?'

'The very same.'

'Oh, I know him – by name that is. Distant relation. My grandmother was an Osten. Isn't he the one who's on a war footing with Bismarck?'

'That's the one. I know what, Wedell, why don't you come along? The Club won't run away, and nor will Pitt and Serge. If they're there at one they'll be there at three. The old boy still has a passion for the blue and gold dragoons and is a Neumark man enough to be delighted to meet a Wedell.'

'Very well, Rienäcker, but on your responsibility.'

'Gladly.'

With these words they arrived at Hiller's, where the old baron was already standing at the glass door looking about him, for it was a minute after one. He made no remark, however, and was visibly pleased when Botho presented his companion: 'Lieutenant von Wedell'.

'Your nephew –'

'No apologies, Herr von Wedell. Anyone who bears the name is a welcome sight to me, and if he wears that uniform, then twice and three times over. Come along, gentlemen, let's extricate ourselves from this table-and-chair formation and see if we can mass our forces at the rear. Not the usual Prussian tactics, but advisable in this instance.'

So saying, he went ahead to find a good table, and after peering into several small rooms finally chose a somewhat larger one with leather-coloured material on the walls, which despite a wide three-framed window had little light because it looked out onto a narrow, dark courtyard. The table was laid for four, but the superfluous setting was cleared away in an instant, and while the two officers placed sword and sabre* by the corner of the window the old baron turned to the head waiter, who had followed at a distance, and ordered lobster and a white burgundy. 'But which one, Botho?'

'Shall we say Chablis?'

'Chablis it is. And some fresh water. But not straight from the tap; I like it when it mists up the carafe. And now, gentlemen, if you'll take your seats: you here, my dear Wedell, and Botho, you over there. If only it weren't for this sweltering heat, these dog days come early. Fresh air, gentlemen, fresh air! This fine Berlin of yours, which is getting finer by the day (at least so we're told by people who don't know any better) – this fine Berlin has everything except fresh air.' And with that he threw open the large middle window panes and then adjusted his position so that he had the wide opening directly in front of him.

The lobster had not yet arrived, but the Chablis was already on the table. With nervous agitation old Osten took a roll from the breadbasket and, just for something to do, cut it hastily but dextrously into diagonal pieces. Then he let the knife fall and extended his hand to Wedell. 'Exceedingly obliged to you, Herr von Wedell, and a brilliant idea of Botho's to tear you away from the Club for a couple of hours. I take it as a good omen that I've had the opportunity to meet a Wedell on my first sortie in Berlin.'

Unable to sit still any longer, he began pouring out the wine. Then he ordered a bottle of Clicquot to be put on ice for them, and continued, 'In fact, my dear Wedell, we're related; there aren't any Wedells that we're not related to,

---

* Botho wears the cuirassiers' broadsword, Wedell the sabre of the dragoons.

though it's remote in some cases. Good Neumark blood in all of 'em. And when I see my old dragoon blue again my heart fairly leaps out of my chest. Yes, Herr von Wedell, old love lies deep. Ah, here comes the lobster ... The large claw there please – the claw's always the best bit ... But what I wanted to say is that old love lies deep, and so do guts. And I might add, thank God for that. In my day we still had old Dobeneck. Now *that*'s what I call a man, dammit! As straight-forward as a child, but if things were going badly and nothing was coming together, the way he'd look at you, I'd like to see the man who could face him. A real old East Prussian who'd been through '13 and '14. We were afraid of him, but we loved him too. He was like a father to us. And do you know, Herr von Wedell, who my captain was ...?'

Just then the champagne arrived.

'Manteuffel, the man we owe everything to, who created our army and in doing so brought us victory.'

Herr von Wedell bowed, while Botho lightly remarked, 'One could say that, certainly.'

It was immediately plain that Botho would have shown more judgement and wisdom by keeping quiet, for the old baron, who suffered from congestion as it was, turned red over the whole of his bald head, while the tufts of frizzy hair above his ears seemed to grow even frizzier. 'I don't under-stand you, Botho. What is "one could say that" supposed to mean? It means that one could also say the opposite. And I know perfectly well what you're driving at. That a certain reserve cuirassier,[*] who hasn't shown much reserve in anything, least of all revolutionary measures – that a certain sulphur-yellow-collared officer garrisoned in Halberstadt

---

[*] The Imperial Chancellor Prince Bismarck, who was a reserve officer of the Halberstadt Cuirassiers and liked to appear in their yellow-trimmed white uniform. In the 1870s Bismarck was still considered a liberal by many of the Prussian nobility.

actually stormed St Privat and encircled Sedan all by himself. Botho, you can't come at me with that. He was once a junior civil servant working for the government in Potsdam, under old Meding, in fact, who I happen to know never had a good word to say about him, and all he ever learnt was how to write despatches. *That* he can do, I'll grant him that; in other words he's a penpusher. But it's not penpushers who made Prussia great. Was the victor of Fehrbellin a penpusher? Or Leuthen? Was Blücher a penpusher, or Yorck? In the Prussian army feathers are for cockades, not for scribbling with. I find this cult unbearable.'

'But my dear Uncle –'

'– Don't "but" me. I won't have any buts. Believe me Botho, you need age and experience for these sorts of questions, and I've got a better understanding of them. What are the facts of the case? He kicks over the ladder that got him to the top, and even bans the *Kreuzzeitung*,* and to put it bluntly he's ruining the old nobility; he looks down on us, insults us to our faces, and when he feels like it he prosecutes us for theft or embezzlement and locks us up in a fortress. No, not a fortress, what am I saying? Fortresses are for respectable people – no, he sends us to the workhouse to pluck wool. But we need some fresh air in here, gentlemen, fresh air! You've got no air in this city. Infernal hole!'

And he got up and tore open the two smaller windows either side of the main one that was already open, with the result that the curtains and tablecloth started flapping in the draught. Returning to his seat, he took a piece of ice from the champagne bucket and rubbed it across his forehead.

'Ah,' he continued, 'this piece of ice here is the best thing about the whole meal ... Now tell me, Herr von Wedell, am I right or not? And Botho, hand on heart, am I right? Isn't it true that any nobleman from the Mark worth his rank must

---

* Newspaper of the conservative interest.

give vent to his indignation, even if he risks being tried for
high treason as a consequence? To think that a man like
Harry von Arnim[*] ... from our best family ... a cut above the
Bismarcks, and so many of them fallen for king and country
that you could make a household company from them, a
company with metal helmets and Boitzenburg-Arnim at their
head. Yes, gentlemen. And for such a family to be insulted
in such a manner. And why? Embezzlement, misconduct,
betrayal of state secrets – I ask you! Why not infanticide and
indecent assault? And truly it's quite surprising that *those*
haven't been tried as well. But you're not saying anything,
gentlemen. Come, come, speak up. Believe me, I'm perfectly
prepared to hear other views. Not like him. Speak up, Herr
von Wedell, speak up.'

Wedell, growing more and more embarrassed, tried to
find some conciliatory words to calm him down. 'To be sure,
Baron, it is as you say. But, if you'll forgive me, at the time the
matter was being decided I heard many people say something
that has stuck in my mind – that the weaker man mustn't
stand in the way of the stronger; it should not be, in politics as
in life. They said there's no denying that might comes before
right.'

'What, without any dissent, any right of appeal?'

'Oh yes, Baron, in some circumstances there is a right
of appeal. And to be perfectly frank with you I know of
cases where opposition was justified. Because what weakness
precludes, purity permits – purity of conviction, integrity of
mind. Then there *is* a right to stand up to authority, a duty
even. But who *has* this integrity? Did ...? But I'll say no
more – I don't wish to offend you, Baron, or the family we're
talking about. But you know, without me saying anything,
that the man who risked this did *not* have such integrity

---

[*] Former German ambassador to Paris who quarrelled with Bismarck. For
more details see 'Historical Persons and Places Mentioned'.

of character. Everything is permitted to the pure at heart; nothing to the merely weak.'

'Everything is permitted to the pure at heart,' repeated the old baron with such a knowing expression on his face that it was unclear whether it was more the truth or the fallacy of the proposition that struck him. 'Everything is permitted to the pure at heart. A capital motto, which I shall take home with me. It will appeal to my parson, who took up arms against me last autumn and attempted to claim a piece of my farmland. Not for his own benefit – oh no, God forbid! – but simply on principle and to make sure he stood up for his successor's interests. Sly old fox. But everything is permitted to the pure at heart.'

'I'm sure you'll give way in the matter of the parson's acre,' said Botho. 'I remember Schönemann from his time with the Sellenthins.'

'Yes, at that time he was a private tutor and liked nothing better than making the lessons shorter and the playtime longer. And he could play hoops like a young marquis; it was a real pleasure to watch him. But he's had his living for seven years now, and you wouldn't recognize him as the Schönemann who used to dance attendance on her ladyship. One thing I must say for him, though, he did a good job of bringing up the two gels, especially your Käthe ...'

Botho gave his uncle a pained look, almost as if to plead for discretion. However, the old baron, jubilant at having seized the ticklish subject so successfully by the forelock, pressed on more keenly and in mounting good humour. 'Bah, discretion! Stuff and nonsense, Botho. Wedell's a Neumark man and he'll know the story as well as anyone else. Why make a big secret of it? You're as good as engaged. And by God, my boy, line up as many gels for inspection as you like, you won't find one to touch her; teeth like pearls and always laughing so that you can see the whole row of 'em. A flaxen-haired beauty made to be kissed, and if I were thirty years younger, you can believe me ...'

Wedell, noticing Botho's discomfort, sought to come to his aid: 'The Sellenthin ladies are all most appealing, mother and daughters; I was with them last summer on Nordeney. All charming, but I would give the palm to the second daughter.'

'So much the better, Wedell, then you won't get in each other's way, and we can celebrate a double wedding. And Schönemann can take it (as long as Kluckhuhn, who's touchy like all old men, allows it), and if the wedding takes place within a year from now I'll give him the use of the carriage and hand over the parson's acre without further ado. You're rich, my dear Wedell, so there's no great hurry for you. But consider our friend Botho here. He doesn't owe his well-nourished appearance to his sandpit of an estate, which aside from a few meadows is really nothing more than a pinery; and even less to his whitefish lake. 'Whitefish lake' – sounds wonderful, almost poetic you might say. But that's *all* you can say for it. You can't live on whitefish. I know you don't like hearing all this, Botho, but now that we're on the subject I must have my say. What's the position, then? Your grandfather sold the heath for a knock-down price, and your late father – a capital fellow, but I've never seen anyone play *l'hombre* that badly or for such high stakes – your late father, I say, divided up the four hundred acres of marshland and sold 'em to the Jeseritz peasants, and the good land left over didn't amount to much, and the thirty thousand thalers he made are long since gone as well. If you were alone it might just do, but you'll have to share it with your brother, and at present it's all still in the hands of your Mama, my good lady sister, a splendid woman, shrewd and sensible, but not exactly the soul of thrift. Botho, it's not for nothing that you're in the Imperial Cuirassiers, and it's not for nothing that you've got a rich cousin who's just waiting for you to come along and clinch things by proposing to her properly and setting the seal on what your parents agreed when you were children. What is there to mull over? Now listen, if I could drop in on your mother on my way home tomorrow and give her the news: "Josephine, my dear, Botho says yes, it's all settled" – now listen, my boy, that would be something to gladden the heart of an old uncle who only wants to see you right. You talk to him, Wedell. It's high time he quitted the single state. Otherwise he'll squander what's left of his fortune or even get hooked by some chit from the bourgeoisie. Am I right? Of course I am. Settled. And now we must drink to it. But not with these dregs ...' And he pressed the bell.

'A Heidsieck. Your best.'

8

AT THAT MOMENT two young gentlemen were sitting together in the Club: one, a Life Guards officer, was tall, slim and clean-shaven; and the other, seconded from the Pasewalk Cuirassiers, somewhat shorter, bearded except for the regulation bare chin. The white damask tablecloth on which they had eaten lunch was folded back, and on the uncovered half of the table they were playing piquet.

'Six cards and a quart.'

'Right.'

'And you?'

'Quatorze of aces, trio of kings, trio of queens ... You won't make a trick.' And he spread his hand on the table and then instantly gathered up the cards for his companion to shuffle.

'Did you know Ella's getting married?'

'Pity.'

'Why so?'

'She won't be able to jump through a hoop any more.'

'Nonsense. The more they marry the slimmer they get.'

'There are exceptions. Many names in the circus aristocracy are still going strong in the third or fourth generation, which rather suggests an alternation between slim and not so slim, or, if you like, between full moon and first quarter.'

'Wrong. *Error in calculo*. You're forgetting adoption. All these circus folk are secret Gichtelians* and bequeath their money, names and reputations according to a set plan. They look the same but really they're different people. Constant new blood. Cut the pack, then ... Anyway, I've got another piece of news. Afzelius is joining the General Staff.'

'Which Afzelius?'

'The lancer.'

'You don't say!'

'Moltke thinks the world of him, and he's supposed to have written a first-rate paper.'

'Doesn't impress me. Just sitting in a library copying things out. Anyone with a bit of ingenuity can turn out books like Humboldt's or Ranke's.'

'Quart. Quatorze of aces.'

'Quint to a king.'

And so trick followed trick, while from the adjoining billiard room came the sound of balls striking one another and little skittles being toppled.

There were altogether only about six or eight men assembled in the two oblong back rooms of the Club that looked out onto a sunny but rather uninteresting garden. All sat quietly, all more or less immersed in their whist or dominoes, not least the two piquet-playing gentlemen who had just been discussing Ella and Afzelius. The stakes were high, and they did not look up from their game until they perceived a new

---

* Followers of the teachings of the German mystic Johann Georg Gichtel (1638-1710). They sought to assuage God's wrath at the sins of mankind by forswearing carnal pleasures and never marrying.

arrival walking through a round-arched opening from the neighbouring back room. It was Wedell.

'Well now, Wedell. It's onto the blacklist with you unless you've brought a whole world of news for us.'

'My apologies, Serge, but it wasn't a definite arrangement.'

'As good as. But speaking for myself, you find me in a very forbearing mood. How you make it up to Pitt, who's just lost a hundred and fifty points, is your affair.'

With that the two men pushed their cards to one side, and the one Wedell had greeted as Serge pulled out his pocket watch: 'Quarter past three. In other words coffee-time. One of the philosophers – surely one of the greatest – once said that the best thing about coffee is that it suits any occasion and any time of day. True and wise words, those. But where shall we take it? I suggest we sit outside on the terrace, right in the sun. The more one braves the weather the better one fares. Right then, Pehlecke, three cups. I can't sit here listening to the billiard skittles being knocked over any more; it's making me nervous. Of course there's noise outside too, but a different kind – instead of this sharp clickety-click we'll hear the rumble and thunder of our underground bowling alley, and we can imagine that we're sitting on Vesuvius or Mount Etna. And why not? Ultimately all pleasures are illusory, and the stronger your imagination the more pleasure you'll have. Only what's unreal has any value and so actually it's the only real thing.'

'Serge,' replied the other piquet-player, who had been addressed as Pitt, 'if you come out with any more of your famous great sayings you'll be punishing Wedell more harshly than he deserves. Besides, as I've lost you ought to take my feelings into consideration. Fine, let's sit here then, with the lawn to the rear, the ivy on our flank, and a blank wall in front of us. A heavenly spot for His Majesty's Guards!

I wonder what old Prince Pückler* would have said to this Club garden. Pehlecke ... that table over here, that's it. And–one last thing–a Havana from your oldest box. And now, Wedell, if you want forgiveness give your sleeve a shake and see if a new war drops out or some other big piece of news. After all, you're related through the Puttkamers to our national divinity. I don't need to say which one. What's he cooking up now?'

'Pitt,' said Wedell, 'no questions about Bismarck, I implore you. For one thing you know I know nothing, as cousins seventeen times removed don't exactly count among his intimates and confidants; and, secondly, I haven't just come from the prince, but straight from a shooting party, with a few hits and far more misses–all aimed at none other than His Excellency himself.'

'And who was this audacious marksman?'

'Old Baron Osten, Rienäcker's uncle. A charming old gentleman and a good sport. But a slyboots with it.'

'Like all natives of the Mark.'

'I'm one too.'

'*Tant mieux*. You've got first-hand proof, then. But come on, out with it. What did the old boy say?'

'All sorts of things. The political stuff hardly worth mentioning, but something else very much so: Rienäcker's in a tight corner.'

'What do you mean?'

'They want him to marry.'

'Is that what you call a tight corner? For goodness' sake, Wedell, Rienäcker's in a much tighter one than that. He's got nine thousand a year and spends twelve. That's the tightest corner there is, certainly a good deal tighter than marriage. For Rienäcker marriage isn't a threat, it's salvation. Besides,

---

* Prince Hermann von Pückler-Muskau (1785–1871), the outstanding German landscape designer of the nineteenth century.

I've seen it coming. And who's it to be, then?'

'A cousin of his.'

'Naturally. Saviours and cousins are almost the same thing these days. And I'll bet she's called Paula. All cousins are called Paula now.'

'Not this one.'

'What then?'

'Käthe.'

'Käthe? Oh, I know. Käthe Sellenthin. Hmm, not bad. Splendid match. Old Sellenthin – it's the one with the eye-patch, isn't it? – he's got six estates, thirteen in fact if you include the farms. All to be divided equally, with the thirteenth going to Käthe as a bonus. Well, hats off ...'

'Do you know her?'

'I certainly do. Wonderful flaxen blonde with eyes like forget-me-nots, but not the sentimental type, more sun than moon. She was a boarder here at Fräulein Zülow's, and at fourteen she already had admirers hovering all around her.'

'What, in boarding-school?'

'Well, not right there and not every day, but on Sundays when old Osten took her out to dine, the same one you've just been with. Käthe, Käthe Sellenthin ... In those days she was like a little wagtail, and that's what we called her. The most delightful filly you could ever imagine. I can still see the way she tied her hair – we called it the distaff. And now it's Rienäcker's job to unwind it. Well, why not? Won't be too much of a hardship for him.'

'Maybe more so that some people realize,' Wedell replied. 'And much as he needs to improve his finances, I'm still not at all sure that he'll plump for his blond-haired regional speciality without further ado. The fact is that for a while now Rienäcker's been familiarizing himself with another hair colour, ash-blond to wit, and if what Balafré told me the other day is true, he's been seriously considering raising up his white linen girl into a white lady – just like the opera.[*] He can imagine that Zehden Manor is his own Avenel Castle, and as you know Rienäcker quite often goes his own way and always had a partiality for naturalness.'

'Yes,' laughed Pitt, 'so he has. But Balafré's dramatizing things and making up entertaining stories. You're a sober man, Wedell, surely you're not going to believe made-up stuff like that.'

'No, not if it is made up,' said Wedell. 'But I believe what I see. For all his six feet, or maybe because of them, Rienäcker's weak-willed and easily led, and unusually soft and kind-hearted.'

'So he is. But circumstances will force his hand, and he'll break away and free himself, if the worst comes to the worst like a fox from a trap. It hurts, and a bit of the stuff of life is left behind. But most of it gets out, and you're free. Long live Käthe! And Rienäcker! What's the old proverb? "God helps those who help themselves."'

9

BOTHO wrote to Lene the same evening that he would come the next day, perhaps a little earlier than usual. He kept his word and arrived an hour before sundown. Naturally Frau Dörr was there too. The air was delicious, not too warm, and after they had chatted awhile Botho said, 'Maybe we should go out into the garden.'

'Yes, the garden, or somewhere else?'

'What do you mean?'

---

[*] François-Adrien Boieldieu's *La Dame blanche* (1825), in which the hero marries an orphan (like Lene) who has helped him secure his rightful inheritance.

Lene laughed. 'You needn't worry, Botho. There's no one lying in ambush, and the lady with the garland and white horses won't step out in front of you.'

'Where then, Lene?'

'Just into the fields, into the country, where you'll have nothing but me and the daisies. And perhaps Frau Dörr as well, if she'll be so good as to accompany us.'

'If she'll be so good,' said Frau Dörr. 'Of course she will! Much honoured, I'm sure. But first I'll have to go and do myself up a bit. I'll be back in a minute.'

'No need, Frau Dörr, we'll come and fetch you.'

And so they did, and as the young couple walked across to the market garden a quarter of an hour later Frau Dörr was already standing at her door with a shawl over her arm and a magnificent hat on her head, the latter a present from Dörr, who, like all misers, occasionally bought something absurdly expensive.

Botho paid her a compliment on her smart appearance, and then all three made their way down the walk and through a small, concealed side-gate onto a field path, which for a short distance skirted the garden fence, overgrown on this outer side with tall nettles, before turning off further down into an open meadow.

'We'll stick to this path,' said Lene. 'It's the prettiest and also the most solitary. No one ever comes this way.'

It was indeed the most solitary path, far more tranquil and deserted than the three or four others that cut parallel with it through the meadow towards Wilmersdorf and, for parts of the way, exhibited some strange forms of suburban life. Running along one of them was a motley collection of sheds connected to each other by metal scaffolds with horizontal bars like those a gymnast might use. This aroused Botho's curiosity, and he was about to ask what it was all for when he got his answer by way of demonstration. Rugs and carpets were spread over the scaffolds and then beaten this way and that with long cane sticks, so that the adjacent path soon lay in a cloud of dust.

Botho pointed this out and was just launching into a conversation with Frau Dörr about the advantages and disadvantages of carpets (which, if you thought about it, were just dust traps, and anyone with a weak chest could get consumption from them in a trice). He broke off in mid-sentence, however, because just then the path they had taken led past what must have been the rubbish dump of a sculptor's workshop, for there were many and various plaster ornaments, especially cherubs' heads, lying around.

'That's a cherub's head,' he said. 'Look, Frau Dörr, and here's one complete with wings.'

'Yes,' responded Frau Dörr. 'An' a real chubby-cheeks too. But is it really a cherub? I thought when they were so small an' with wings they were called cupids.'

'Oh, cupids and cherubs, it's the same thing,' said Botho. 'Just ask Lene, she'll back me up. Isn't that so, Lene?'

Lene looked hurt, but he took her hand and everything was all right again.

Directly behind the rubbish dump the path bent round to the left and joined a somewhat wider country lane lined with blossoming black poplars that strewed their fleecy catkins over the meadow like tufts of cotton wool.

'Look, Lene,' said Frau Dörr, 'did you know they stuff beds with it now, jus' like with feathers? An' they call it tree wool.'

'Yes, Frau Dörr, I know. And I'm always glad when people make a discovery like that and put it to good use. But it wouldn't suit you, I don't think.'

'No, Lene, not a bit it wouldn't. You're right there. I like it nice an' firm, horsehair an' springs, so that if you really toss up and down ...'

'Of course, yes,' said Lene, anxious at the turn this description was taking. 'But I'm afraid we might get some rain. Just listen to the frogs, Frau Dörr.'

'Oh, the puddocks,' the latter agreed. 'Some nights they croak so much you can't get no sleep. And do you know why? 'cos it's really one big marsh round here, an' only looks like a meadow. Just look at that bog pool, where that stork's standin' an' starin' across at us. Well, it's not me he's lookin' at. Wouldn't make no difference if it was, I'm glad to say.'

'We really ought to be turning back,' said Lene, in her embarrassment speaking the first words that came to mind.

'Course not,' laughed Frau Dörr. 'Not when we've got this far. You won't be scared, Lene, surely, not of somethin' like that. *Mr Stork, my good friend, bring me* ... Or is it *Mr Stork, my best friend* ...?'

And so she went on, for it always took Frau Dörr a while to relinquish a pet subject such as this.

At last she fell silent and they walked on at a slow pace until they reached a ridge of high ground that formed a plateau connecting the Spree and the Havel. This was where the meadow ended, to be succeeded by fields of corn and rape that ran all the way to the first row of houses in Wilmersdorf.

'Let's just get up there,' said Frau Dörr, 'and then we'll sit down and pick some buttercups and tie 'em into a necklace. Lord, it's always such fun threadin' the stems together till you've got a necklace or a chain.'

'Right you are,' said Lene, whose fate it was today to suffer one awkward moment after another. 'Right you are. Come along now, Frau Dörr, the path goes this way.'

And they climbed up the gentle slope and then sat down at the top on a heap of lousewort and nettles that people had been dumping there since the previous autumn. This heap was a splendid resting-place, and also a vantage-point overlooking a canal flanked by various species of willow and, beyond it, the northernmost row of houses in Wilmersdorf, while from a nearby bowling tavern came the distinct sound of the skittles being toppled and especially the bowls rolling back alongside the lanes on two rickety slats. Lene, thoroughly delighted by it all, took Botho's hand and said, 'You know, Botho, I'm a proper expert on this because when I was a child we lived next to a bowling tavern, and I only have to hear the ball hit the floor to know what it will score.'

'Well,' said Botho, 'let's bet on it.'

'What shall we bet?'

'We'll think of something.'

'Fine. But I only have to get it right three times, and if I say nothing it doesn't count.'

'Sounds fair.'

And so all three strained their ears, and Frau Dörr, growing more excited with each moment, swore by everything sacred that her heart was thumping and that she felt just like before curtain-up in the theatre. 'Lene, Lene, you've asked too much of yourself, my dear girl, it's jus' not possible.'

She would probably have said more had they not just heard a ball being released and then hitting the side wall before falling silent. 'Miss!' cried Lene. And she was right.

'That was easy,' said Botho. 'Too easy. I'd have guessed that too. Let's see what comes next.'

And behold, two more rolls followed without Lene saying a word or even stirring, while Frau Dörr's eyes protruded more and more from their sockets. But now – and Lene shot up from where she was sitting – they heard a small, firmly bowled ball dance along the boards with a peculiar vibrating tone that combined hardness and elasticity. 'All nine!' cried Lene. An instant later the skittles were scattered, and though it hardly needed stating the skittles boy confirmed the score.

'Let's declare you the winner, Lene. Tonight we'll eat a Vielliebchen,* and there'll be nothing left to wish for. Isn't

---

* Dinner-table custom whereby a nut with a double-kernel was shared by a man and a woman. When they next met the first to say 'Good morning, Vielliebchen [well-beloved]' could demand a small gift, usually a kiss.

that right, Frau Dörr?'

'Course,' said the latter, winking, 'nothin' left to wish for.' And she untied her hat and spun it around as if it were the one she wore to market.

Meanwhile the sun was sinking behind the Wilmersdorf church steeple, and Lene proposed that as it was getting chilly they should get moving again for home; on the way they could play tag, and she was sure Botho wouldn't be able to catch her.

'Well, we'll see about that!'

But despite all the chasing and snatching that followed Lene did indeed evade capture, until at last she was so weak with laughter and excitement that she took refuge behind the imposing figure of Frau Dörr.

'Now I've found myself a tree,' she laughed, 'so you definitely won't get me.' And she clung to the tails of Frau Dörr's loose-fitting jacket and pushed the good woman right and left so skilfully that for a while she succeeded in shielding herself. But then suddenly Botho was beside her, holding her fast and giving her a kiss.

'That's against the rules. We didn't agree to that.' But she belied her own rebuff by hanging on his arm. Then, imitating a drill-sergeant's snarl, she commanded, 'Atten*tion* ... quick march', and was highly amused at the endless stream of admiring exclamations that their play elicited from the good Frau Dörr.

'Would you believe it?' said the latter. 'No you would *not*. And like this all the time, and never any different. An' when I think of mine! Just unbelievable. An' yet he was one too, with the same way about him.'

'What's she talking about?' asked Botho softly.

'Oh, she's thinking back ... You know ... I told you about it.'

'Oh *that*. Him. Well, he can't have been all that bad, I don't suppose?'

'Who knows? I suppose one's much the same as another.'

'You think?'

'No.' She shook her head, and a soft tenderness shone from her eyes. But she did not want to let this feeling gain on her, and so she hastily said, 'A song, Frau Dörr, let's have a song. But what shall it be?'

'*At dawn's first flush ...*'

'No, not that ... It ends with *To the cold grave tomorrow*, and that's too sad for me. No, let's sing *A year from now, a year from now*, or, even better, *Do you still remember?**'

'Yes, that's a good one, that's nice. It's my favourite of all.'

And with well-practised voices all three sang Frau Dörr's favourite song, and as they approached the market garden the words *Oh I still remember ... I owe my life to you* were still ringing out across the fields and then echoing back from the long row of sheds and storehouses that bordered the next path.

Frau Dörr was overjoyed, but Lene and Botho had grown solemn.

10

IT WAS ALREADY GETTING DARK by the time they reached Frau Nimptsch's house, and Botho, who had soon recovered his cheerful spirits, intended to look in just for a moment before saying goodbye. However, when Lene reminded him of various promises he had made and Frau Dörr, with emphasis and a meaningful rolling of her eyes, of the Vielliebchen still to be eaten, he yielded and decided to stay for the evening.

'That's right,' said Frau Dörr. 'And then I'll stay too – if I

---

* Song by Wilhelm Hauff (1824), folk-song, and duet from Karl von Holtei's play *Der alte Feldherr* (*The Old General*, 1829).

may, that is, an' if I won't disturb the Vielliebchen. 'cos you never know. But I must just take my hat back home, and my shawl. And then I'll be back.'

'Of course you must come back,' said Botho, giving her his hand. 'We won't be this young when we meet again.'

'No, no,' laughed Frau Dörr, 'we won't be this young when we meet again. And there's no way we could be, even if we meet again tomorrow. 'cos a day's still a day and makes a difference. And so you're quite right that we won't be this young when we meet again. And we'll all just have to accept it.'

She went on for a while in this vein, and the undisputed fact of the daily ageing process struck her so forcefully that she repeated it a few more times. Finally she left, and Lene accompanied her into the hallway. Meanwhile Botho sat down beside Frau Nimptsch and, adjusting the wrap that had slipped from her shoulders, asked if she was angry that he had stolen Lene from her again for a couple of hours. But it had been so lovely, he said, and sitting on the heap of lousewort they had rested and chatted and completely forgotten the time.

'Yes, when you're happy you do forget the time,' said the old woman. 'And young people are happy, which is just as it should be. But when you get old, dear Herr Baron, time starts to drag, and you wish the days would end an' your life too.'

'Oh, you're just saying that, mother. Everyone loves life, old or young. That's right, isn't it, Lene, we all love life?'

Lene had just stepped back from the hallway into the living room, and when she heard Botho's words she was as if electrified. In a display of passion very unlike her usual self she ran up, threw her arms around his neck and kissed him.

'Lene, whatever's the matter?'

But she had already composed herself, and warded off his concern with a quick wave of her hand, as if to say 'Don't ask.' And now, while Botho continued talking to Frau Nimptsch, she went over to the kitchen cupboard, rummaged around, and then came back, smiling brightly, with a booklet sewn into blue sugar-bag paper covers which exactly resembled those in which housewives note down their daily expenses. Such was this booklet's purpose too, but it also contained some questions which, whether from general curiosity or some deeper interest, were on Lene's mind. She opened it at the last page, where Botho's eye immediately lighted on the heavily underlined heading *Things I Need to Know*.

'Gracious me, Lene, that sounds like a little tract or the title of a comedy.'

'It is in a way. Read on.'

And he read: 'Who were the two ladies at the Korso? Is it the older one or the younger one? Who is Pitt? Who is Serge? Who is Gaston?'

Botho laughed. 'If I answered all that, Lene, I'd be here till morning.'

It was fortunate that Frau Dörr was not present to hear this, otherwise there would have been another awkward moment. But their friend, usually so quick off the mark – at least where the baron was concerned – had still not returned, and so Lene said: 'All right, I'll agree on this. We can talk about the two ladies another time. But what do the foreign names mean? I asked you this not long ago, when you brought the bag of crackers, but what you said wasn't a proper answer, or only half of one. Is it a secret?'

'No.'

'Tell me then.'

'Gladly, Lene. They're just nicknames.'

'I know. You said that before.'

'... in other words, names we give each other just for convenience. Sometimes there's an association, but not always.'

'So what does Pitt mean?'

'Pitt was an English statesman.'

'And is your friend one too?'

'Good heavens ...'

'And Serge?'

'That's a Russian Christian name. There was a saint called Serge, and lots of Russian Grand Dukes.'

'Not necessarily saintly. Am I right? ... And Gaston?'

'A French name.'

'Yes, I can remember that. When I was very young, before I was even confirmed, I saw a play called *The Man in the Iron Mask*. And the character with the mask was called Gaston. And I cried my eyes out.'

'Well, you'll laugh now, because *I'm* Gaston.'

'No I won't. You've got a mask on as well.'

Botho wanted, half in jest and half in earnest, to assert the opposite, but the conversation was cut short at that moment by the reappearance of Frau Dörr, who apologized for keeping them waiting for so long. An order had just come in, she said, and she'd quickly had to make up a funeral wreath.

'A big one or a small one?' asked Frau Nimptsch, who had a passion for talking about funerals or hearing any information about them.

'Oh, middling,' said Frau Dörr. 'Simple folk. Ivy with azaleas.'

'Lord,' continued Frau Nimptsch, 'everyone wants ivy with azaleas nowadays, not me though. Ivy's all right when it grows over the top of the grave, all green and thick like a blanket to protect it and the person underneath. But ivy in a wreath, that's not right. In my day we used immortelles, yellow or cream ones, or, for somethin' really special, red or white – sometimes we'd make several wreaths, or just one to hang over the cross, and then it'd last all winter and still be there when spring came. Even longer sometimes. But ivy with azaleas is no good. You know why? 'cos it doesn't last. I always think: the longer a wreath lasts, the longer someone's thinkin' of the person that's died. Includin' widows, as long as they're not too young. And that's why I prefer immortelles, yellow or red ones or white, an' anyone can add another wreath if they want – jus' for the look of the thing. Yes, immortelles are the right thing.'

'Mother,' said Lene, 'there you go again talking about graves and wreaths.'

'Yes, child, we all talk about what's on our minds. If it's a weddin' we talk about weddin's, an' if it's a funeral we talk about graves and wreaths. An' it wasn't me as brought the subject up; it was Frau Dörr, which is only right an' proper. And the only reason I keep on about it is that I'm always afraid when I think: who's goin' to bring me one?'

'Oh, mother . . .'

'Yes, Lene, you're a good, kind girl. But Man proposes, God disposes; an' here today and gone tomorrow. An' you could die jus' as well as me, any day that God sends, although I don't really believe it. And Frau Dörr could die too, or when I die she might be livin' somewhere else, or I'm livin' somewhere else and maybe only jus' moved in. Ah, my own dear Lene, there's nothin' certain in this life, nothin' at all, not even a wreath on your own grave.'

'Ah, Mother Nimptsch,' said Botho, 'that's one thing that *is* certain.'

'Well, well, Herr Baron, I only hope you're right.'

'And even if I'm in St Petersburg or Paris and I hear that my old Frau Nimptsch has died, I'll send a wreath; and if I'm in Berlin or nearby I'll bring it myself.'

The old woman's face was quite suffused with joy. 'Well, Herr Baron, there's a promise. And now I've got a wreath on my grave after all, an' I'm so glad that I have. 'cos I can't stand bare graves – looks like an orphanage cemetery or one for prisoners or even worse. But now go an' make some tea, Lene, the kettle's already boilin' and bubblin', an' there's strawberries and cream there too. Sour cream as well. Lord, the poor Herr Baron must be all famished. Starin' at someone for hours makes you hungry – that much I do remember. Yes, Frau Dörr, we were all young once, even if it was a long time ago. But people were the same then as what they are now.'

Frau Nimptsch had clearly oiled her tongue today, and she continued philosophizing for a while as Lene served the supper and Botho resumed his teasing of Frau Dörr. A good thing she had put her best hat away safely, he told her; a hat like that was fine for the Kroll Gardens or the theatre, but not for a lousewort heap outside Wilmersdorf. Where had she got it from? Even princesses didn't have hats like that. He declared he'd never seen anything as becoming in his life, and she might easily make a conquest of a royal prince – to say nothing of himself.

The good woman could see perfectly well that he was having his joke. Even so she replied, 'Yes, Dörr does have his moments, and then he's so gallant and stylish that it sometimes mystifies me where he gets it from. Normally he's not up to much, but in a flash it comes over him an' he's like a different man, and then I always say: maybe there's somethin' to him after all, and he's just no good at showin' it.'

They carried on drinking tea and chatting until nearly ten o'clock. Then Botho got up to leave, and Lene and Frau Dörr accompanied him through the front garden as far as the gate. As they stood there Frau Dörr reminded them that they had forgotten the Vielliebchen. However, Botho seemed intent on passing this over and instead reaffirmed what a lovely afternoon it had been. 'We must have more outings like that, Lene, and next time I come we'll consider where to go. Oh, I'll think of somewhere all right, somewhere pretty and secluded, and a bit further away, not just across a few fields.'

'And we'll take Frau Dörr again too,' said Lene, 'or ask if she'll come. Won't we, Botho?'

'Certainly, Lene, Frau Dörr must always come too. Nothing doing without Frau Dörr.'

'Oh, Herr Baron, I really can't allow that. I could never

make demands like that.'

'Of course you could, my dear Frau Dörr,' said Botho laughingly. 'A woman like you. There's *nothing* you couldn't demand.'

And with that they parted.

11

FOR SEVERAL WEEKS after the walk to Wilmersdorf the excursion that had been arranged or at least envisaged on that day became a favourite subject of conversation, and each time Botho visited the question was discussed *where to?* All possible destinations were considered: Erkner and Kranichberge, Schwilow and Baumgartenbrück, but all dismissed as being too frequented, until eventually Botho named Hankel's Stowage, saying he had heard marvellous reports of its beauty and solitude. Lene agreed; all she wanted was to get out into the open country, as far as possible from the bustle of the city, and be with the man she loved. It did not matter where.

They fixed on the following Friday for the trip: 'Settled.' And when it came they took the afternoon Görlitz train to Hankel's Stowage, where they intended to stay the night and then pass the next day in complete peace.

The train had only a few carriages, and even these were sparsely filled, so Botho and Lene found that they could sit alone. The people in the next compartment were engaged in an animated conversation, and it could clearly be heard from what they said that they were bound for a destination further down the line than Hankel's Stowage.

Lene was happy; she put her hand in Botho's and gazed silently out of the window at the landscape of woods and heath. After a while she said, 'I wonder what Frau Dörr will say to us leaving her at home?'

'She mustn't hear about it.'

'Mother's bound to blurt it out.'

'Well, that'll be awkward, but there was no other way of doing it. You see, on the meadow the other week it was all right because we didn't meet a soul. But however much solitude we find at Hankel's Stowage there'll still be a landlord and a landlady, and maybe even a Berlin waiter. And a Berlin waiter who's always stifling a smile or at least smiling inwardly would be more than I could endure, it would spoil the pleasure for me. Frau Dörr's priceless when she's sitting next to your mother or telling old Dörr what to do, but not among strangers. Among strangers she's just a figure of fun and an embarrassment.'

At about five o'clock the train halted at the edge of some woods. As they had foreseen, Botho and Lene were the only ones to get out, and they strolled contentedly and with frequent pauses towards an inn situated right on the Spree about ten minutes from the small station building. This 'establishment', as it was named on a lopsided signpost, had originally been a simple fisherman's cottage, and, more by addition than renovation, had very gradually been transformed into an inn. However, the view over the river compensated for any possible shortcomings, so that the excellent reputation this place enjoyed among the initiated did not for a moment seem unmerited. Lene immediately felt at home and settled herself in a veranda-like wooden annexe at the front, half of which was covered by the branches of an old elm that stood between the building and the river bank.

'Let's stay here,' she said. 'Look at those boats, two, three of them ... and there, further up, a whole flotilla coming this way. What a good idea it was for us to come here. Just look at them over there, how they're running up and down the boats and working the oars. And yet everything's so quiet. Oh my own darling Botho, how beautiful it all is, and how much I love you.'

Botho was glad to see Lene so happy. It was as if the resolute, almost astringent element normally present in her character had fallen away and an unwonted gentleness taken its place, and this change appeared to do her a world of good.

After a while the landlord, who had inherited the 'establishment' from his father and grandfather, came to ask if the lady and gentleman wished to order anything, and especially if they were staying for the night. When they answered in the affirmative he asked them to decide which room they would like, and said there were several at their disposal, of which the attic room was probably the best. It had a low ceiling, he said, but otherwise was large and spacious and had a view over the Spree all the way to the Müggel Hills.

When they accepted his suggestion the landlord went off to make the necessary arrangements, and Botho and Lene, alone again, luxuriated in the full happiness of their joint solitude. A finch nesting in some low bushes nearby balanced on one of the elm's drooping branches, swallows darted back and forth, and after a few minutes a black duck made her way past the veranda with a long train of ducklings and then strutted solemnly towards a landing-stage built far out into the river. Halfway along this she came to a stop and the ducklings plunged into the water and paddled away.

Lene watched all this with rapt attention. 'Just look, Botho, see how the current rushes past the posts.' In fact it was neither the landing-stage nor the fast-flowing water that fascinated her, but the two boats chained up at the front. She kept eyeing them and indulging in little questions and hints, and only when Botho turned a deaf ear and quite refused to grasp her meaning did she resort to plain language and declare that she would like to go on the water.

'Women really are incorrigible! Incorrigible in their frivolity. Think of that Easter Monday. You were within an ace –'

'– of drowning. I know. But that was only the first thing. Then I made the acquaintance of a fine-looking gentleman. Perhaps you remember him; his name was Botho ... I hope you're not going to think of that Easter Monday as an unlucky day. I'm more civil and gallant than you there.'

'All right, all right ... But can you actually row, Lene?'

'Of course I can. And I can even steer and set a sail. Just because I was nearly drowned you think badly of me and my skills. But the boy was to blame, and anyway, anyone can drown.'

And with that she went down from the veranda and along the landing-stage to the two boats, whose sails were reefed, the pennants with stitched-on names fluttering from the mastheads.

'Which shall we take,' said Botho, 'the *Trout* or the *Hope*?'

'The *Trout* of course. What's the use of hope to us?'

Botho could tell that Lene said this deliberately to taunt him, for despite the delicacy of her feelings she was still a typical child of Berlin in her liking for pointed remarks. But he forgave this pointedness, and without replying helped her climb in. Then he jumped in after her. Just as he was about to cast off the landlord came over with a jacket and a plaid blanket, saying that it would get cold when the sun went down. They thanked him, and soon afterwards were in the middle of the river, which at this point was pinched by islands and tongues of land and probably not even three hundred paces across. Lene only pulled at the oars intermittently, but even these few strokes sufficed to carry them in a short while to a meadow in tall grass that also served as a boatyard. A little way away men were building a Spree flatboat and caulking and tarring some leaky old craft.

'Let's go over there!' cried Lene gaily, and she pulled Botho along with her. But before they reached the workshop the hammering of the carpenter's axe ceased and the bell began to ring for the end of the working day. So a hundred paces from the boatyard they turned into a path that cut diagonally across the meadow towards a pinewood. The russet trunks glowed magnificently in the rays of the already low sun, and a bluish mist floated above the treetops.

'I'd like to pick you a really fine posy,' said Botho, taking Lene's hand. 'But look, the whole meadow's just grass and no flowers. Not a single one.'

'There are flowers everywhere! You don't see any because you're too choosy.'

'Well, if so it's only for you that I am.'

'Come on, no excuses. Just see, I'll find some.'

And she bent down and searched right and left. 'Look, here's one ... and there ... and here again. There are more here than in Dörr's garden; you just have to have an eye for them.' And she went to work with eager dexterity, pulling up all sorts of weeds and blades of grass at the same time, and in no time she had an armful of matter, both usable and useless.

Presently they came upon a fisherman's hut that had stood empty for years. In front of it, on a strip of sand strewn with pine cones from the woods rising up directly behind, lay an overturned rowing boat.

'This'll suit us admirably,' said Botho, 'let's sit down here. You must be tired. And now show me what you've picked. I believe you don't know yourself, and I'll have to put on my botanist's hat. Let me have them. That's a buttercup, and that's hawkweed, which some people call false forget-me-not. False, mark you. And this one here with notched leaves, that's taraxacum, our good old dandelion, which the French use to make salads. Well, that's their affair. But there's a difference between a salad and a bouquet.'

'You just give them back,' said Lene laughingly. 'You've got no eye for these things because you've got no love for them, and the eye and the heart always go together. First you say there are no flowers in the meadow, and now that we've found some you say they're not proper flowers. But they *are* flowers, and very nice ones too. What do you bet that I can't make you something pretty with them?'

'I must say I'm curious to see what you'll choose.'

'Only ones you agree to yourself. And now let's begin. This one's a forget-me-not, but not the hawkweed kind, not false that is, but a real one. Agreed?'

'Yes.'

'And this one's a speedwell, a graceful little flower. You'll let that count too, won't you? I don't even need to ask. And this big reddish-brown one, that's a devil's bit, your own signature flower. You can laugh all you like ... And these here,' and she bent down over a few small yellow flowers blossoming in the sandy ground right in front of her, 'these are immortelles.'

'Immortelles,' said Botho. 'They're old Frau Nimptsch's passion. Well, we must take those. It wouldn't do to leave them out. And now bind the posy together for me.'

'Right, but what with? Let's wait till we find some reeds.'

'No, I can't wait that long. Besides, a reed isn't good enough; it's too thick and coarse, and I'd like something finer. I know what, Lene, you've got such lovely long hair; pull out a strand and tie the posy up with that.'

'No,' she said firmly.

'No? Why not? Why do you say no?'

'Because the proverb says *Hair binds for ever*. And if I bind a hair round the posy I'll be binding you with it.'

'Bah, that's superstition. That's something Frau Dörr would say.'

'No, it's mother that says it. And whatever she told me from when I was small was always right, even if it sounded like superstition.'

'Well, all right then. I won't argue. But the only ribbon I want round the posy is a hair of yours, and surely you won't be so stubborn as to refuse me that.'

She looked at him, pulled a hair from her parting and wound it round the posy. Then she said: 'Let it be as you wish. Here, take it. Now you're bound too.'

He tried to laugh, but her seriousness of tone, especially in these last words, did not fail to make an impression on him.

'It's getting cool,' he remarked after a few moments. 'The landlord did right to bring you a jacket and blanket. Come on, let's make a move.'

And so they returned to where they had left the boat and hastened back to the other side of the river.

It was only on this second crossing that the inn, to which each stroke of the oar brought them closer, revealed itself in all its picturesqueness to their eyes. The tall thatched roof sat like some bizarre cap on the squat half-timbered building, whose four small front windows were just being illuminated. Just then a few storm lanterns were carried out into the veranda, and through the branches of the old elm, which in the darkness resembled a kind of fantastical trelliswork, beams of light flashed out in various directions over the river.

Neither of them said anything. They mused on their happiness and wondered how much longer it would last.

12

NIGHT was already falling by the time they landed.

'Let's take this table,' said Botho as they stepped back onto the veranda. 'You'll be out of the wind here, and I'll order you a grog or some mulled wine, shall I? I can see you're cold.'

He suggested various other things, but Lene asked if she might go to their room. By the time he came up she'd be feeling better, she said; she was just worn out, that was all, and the only thing she needed was a little rest.

With that she left him and climbed the stairs to the attic

room, which in the meantime had been made ready for them. She was accompanied by the inquisitive landlady, who, having jumped to quite the wrong conclusions, immediately asked what the matter was, and without waiting for an answer carried on: Yes, that's how it was with young women; she knew from experience, and before her eldest was born – she had four now and it would have been five, but the middle one had come early and not lived long – well, she'd had it too. It came on all of a sudden and you felt like death. But a cup of mint tea – proper Carmelite mint tea – soon got rid of it, and in no time you felt as right as rain and all happy and cheerful, and quite in the mood. 'Take it from me, madam, once you've got four of 'em around you, not counting the little angel ...'

Lene struggled to conceal her embarrassment, and just for something to say asked for a cup of mint tea – Carmelite mint tea, which she said she'd heard of too.

While this conversation was taking place in the attic room, Botho had taken a seat, not on the wind-sheltered veranda, but in front of it at a rustic table of rough boards nailed onto four posts, from which he had an unimpeded view. Here, he decided, he would have his dinner. He ordered fish, and when the 'tench with dill' that the inn had long been famous for was served, the landlord came over to ask which wine the Herr Baron (a title he threw out speculatively) would like to choose.

'Well,' said Botho, 'I think the best thing with this delicate tench would be a Brauneberger or, better still, a Rüdesheimer, and as a vote of confidence in its quality you must sit here as my guest and drink your own wine with me.'

The landlord smiled and bowed, and soon returned with a slightly dust-coated bottle, while the serving maid, a pretty Sorbian girl in a frieze skirt and a black headscarf, brought the glasses out on a tray.

'Now, let me see,' said Botho. 'The bottle looks very promising. Too much dust and cobwebs is always suspicious, but this one here ... Ah, superb! A '70 vintage. Am I right? And now let's drink a toast. Right, but to what? I know, to Hankel's Stowage – long may it prosper!'

The landlord was visibly gratified, and Botho, who saw what a good impression he was making, accordingly continued in the easy, affable tone so characteristic of him: 'I think this is a delightful spot; in fact there's only one thing to be said against Hankel's Stowage, and that's the name.'

'Yes,' agreed the landlord, 'the name leaves a lot to be desired and it's actually a bit of a liability for us. And yet there is a reason for it, because Hankel's Stowage really was a stowage, and that's where it got the name from.'

'Fine, but that doesn't get us very far. Why was it called Stowage? What is a stowage?'

'Well, put it this way: a loading and unloading point. For a long time the whole of this area,' and he gestured to his rear, 'was crown land, and under Frederick the Great, and even before that under the Soldier King,[*] it was called the Wusterhausen Estate. It was big, and there were getting on for thirty villages belonging to it, together with woods and heath. And as you can imagine, those thirty villages naturally produced things and needed to get things in, or, to put it another way, there was traffic in and out, and so from the outset they needed a docking and storage place, and the only question was which spot they'd choose. Well, they chose *this* one. This inlet became a harbour, a storage place, a "stowage" for everything that came and went, and because the fisherman who lived here at that time – my ancestor, as it happens – was called Hankel, so it became Hankel's Stowage.'

'What a pity,' said Botho, 'that not everyone can hear that neat and simple explanation.' The landlord, very likely

---

* Frederick William I of Prussia (ruled 1713-40), who carried out administrative reforms and improved army efficiency. Frederick II ('the Great') was his son.

emboldened by these words, was about to continue, but before he could do so they heard a bird call high in the sky, and when Botho looked up curiously he could just discern two huge birds flying above the river and disappearing into the dusk.

'Were those wild geese?'

'No, herons. The whole woodland round here is full of them. In fact it's a real hunting ground, with wild boar and fallow deer galore, and in the reeds and rushes there's duck, snipe and woodcock.'

'Splendid!' said Botho, who felt the huntsman stirring within him. 'You know, I envy you. What does the name matter in the end? Duck, snipe, woodcock – it makes me wish I could have enjoyed a life like this. Only it must be solitary here, too solitary.'

The landlord smiled to himself, and Botho, noticing this, became curious: 'You're smiling, but isn't it true, then? For the last half-hour I've heard nothing except the water gurgling around the landing-stage, and just now the heron's call overhead. I'd say that was solitary, pretty though it is. And occasionally a few big Spree flatboats pass by, but they're all the same or at least look the same. And anyway they're all like ghost ships. It's a real deathly silence.'

'Certainly,' said the landlord. 'But only as long as it lasts.'

'How so?'

'Yes, as long as it lasts,' repeated the other. 'You speak of solitude, Herr Baron, and for days that's just what we have. Weeks sometimes. But as soon as the ice breaks up and spring comes the visitors arrive, and the Berliners are with us.'

'When do they come?'

'Incredibly early. The third Sunday of Lent they start arriving. You know, Herr Baron, I'm really quite hardened to the weather, but while I'm still keeping indoors in my parlour because there's an east wind blowing and a blinding March sun, the Berliners are already sitting out in the open, folding their summer coats over their chairs and ordering themselves

wheat beers. Because as long as the sun's shining they call
it a beautiful day, and don't care if there's pneumonia and
diphtheria lurking with every gust of wind. For them it's just
the time to be playing hoops – or bowls, some of them – and it
makes my heart bleed sometimes to see them when they set
off back home again, all puffy-faced from the baking sun, and
not one of them that isn't at least going to have his skin peel
off in strips the next day.'

Botho laughed. 'That sounds like Berliners! Which
reminds me, isn't it somewhere on this stretch of the Spree
that the oarsmen and yachtsmen get together and have their
regattas?'

'Oh yes,' said the landlord, 'but they're fairly small affairs.
Fifty's a good showing, and now and again they might just
get a hundred. And then it goes quiet again and there are no
more water sports of any kind for weeks and months. No,
those boat club people are relatively easy to deal with and not
too much of a strain. It's when the steamers start coming in
June that it gets bad. And then it stays that way for the whole
summer, or at least for a long, long time.'

'I can believe it,' said Botho.

'... Then every evening we get a telegram: "Tomorrow
9 a.m. Spree steamer *Alsen*. Day trip. 240 people", followed
by the names of the organizers. Once in a while it would
be fine, but after a time it's just too much. Because what do
they do on these trips? Until it gets dark they're out in the
woods and meadows, but then it's time for dinner, and then
there's dancing till eleven. Now you might say that doesn't
sound too bad, and you'd be right if we had the next day off.
But the second day's like the first, and the third day's like
the second. Every night at eleven a steamer with 240 people
leaves, and every morning at nine another steamer with the
same number arrives. And in the meantime everything has
to be tidied up and set to rights. And so we spend the night
ventilating, cleaning and scrubbing, and by the time we've

polished the last door handle the next boat's already here. Of course there's a good side to it as well, and when we count the takings at midnight we know what it's all been for. "From nothing comes nothing", as the old saying goes, and it's quite true; and if I wanted to fill the punchbowls with all the punch that's been drunk here I'd need to fetch the Heidelberg Barrel. It does bring money in, for sure, and that's all well and good. But what you gain in that department you lose in another by paying with your life and health – the most precious things you've got. After all, what's life without sleep?'

'Well,' said Botho, 'I can see there's no such thing as perfect happiness. But when it's winter again you can go into hibernation.'

'Yes, unless it happens to be New Year's Eve or Epiphany or Shrovetide. And they come round more often than you'd think from looking at the calendar. And you should see the hordes of people here then, all arriving by sleigh or on skates from ten different villages and meeting up in the big hall I built as an annexe. We don't get any city faces then, the Berliners leave us in peace; then it's the farmhands and serving maids who have their day, and we see otterskin caps and corduroy jackets with embossed silver buttons. And all sorts of soldiers on leave: Schwedt Dragoons, Fürstenwald Lancers, or even Potsdam Hussars. And they're all jealous and quarrelsome, and it's hard to know what they like better, having a dance or kicking up a row; at the slightest provocation the villages square up to each other and start pitched battles, and they keep up their shouting and rampaging all night long, whole mountains of pancakes just vanish, and it's daybreak by the time they're off again over the frozen river or through the snow back to their homes.'

'Well,' Botho laughed, 'I can see I was wide of the mark talking about solitude and deathly silence. It's lucky I didn't know any of what you've just said, otherwise I'd never have dared come, and I'd be sorry to have missed the chance to see such a pretty corner of the world ... But a moment ago you said "What's life without sleep?", and I can feel myself agreeing with you. I'm tired even though it's still quite early, I suppose because of the fresh air and being on the water. And I must also go and see ... Your dear wife has taken so much trouble ... Good night, landlord, I've chatted on too long.' And with that he rose and made his way to the now silent house.

Lene had reclined on the bed with her feet resting on a chair she had pulled up and drunk a cup of the tea that the landlady had brought her. The peace and warmth did her good and made the weakness she had felt pass away, and after a short while she could easily have gone back down to the veranda and joined in the conversation Botho was having with the landlord. But she did not feel like talking, and so she got up simply to look round the room, to which she had not yet paid any attention.

It was well worth it. The original exposed beams and loam walls had been retained, and the whitewashed ceiling hung so low that she could have touched it with her fingers, but all the improvements it was possible to make had been made. The little windowpanes that still remained on the ground floor had been replaced here by a single large window that almost reached down to the floorboards and provided, just as the landlord said, a splendid view of the surrounding landscape of trees and water. Nor was this large picture window all that modernity and comfort had done for the room. There were also a few good pictures, presumably acquired at auction, hanging amid the many bulges and blisters of the old loam walls, and a pair of elegant dressing-tables stood facing one another just inside the side walls of the projecting window gable, in other words where these walls met the sloping ceiling of the room itself. Everything indicated that when the fishermen's and sailors' tavern had been converted into a pleasant guesthouse for wealthy sportsmen from the local yachting and rowing club its original character had been carefully preserved.

To Lene's eyes there was something appealingly homely about it all, and she now began to take a closer look at the two wide-framed pictures hanging to her right and left above the bedposts. They were engravings, and she was so intrigued by the scenes they depicted that she would have liked to know the meaning of the English captions underneath. 'Washington Crossing the Delaware' stood under one, 'The Last Hour at Trafalgar' under the other. But she could do no more than combine the letters into syllables, and, trivial as the matter was, it nonetheless gave her a pang by bringing home to her the gulf that separated her from Botho. He might scoff at learning and intellect, but she was perceptive enough to know what to make of such scoffing.

Close to the bedroom door, above a rococo table bearing a carafe of water and some red glasses, hung a brightly coloured lithograph with a caption in three languages: *Si jeunesse savait.** She recalled seeing the picture in the Dörrs' house, for Dörr liked that kind of thing. The sight of it again here upset her and made her recoil, her delicate sensuality offended by the image's lewdness as if by a travesty of her own feelings, and to shake off the impression she went over to the gable window and opened both casements to let in the night air. Ah, how refreshing it was! She sat on the windowsill, less than a foot above the floor, wound her left arm round the mullion, and listened for sounds coming from the veranda a short distance away. But she heard nothing. A complete silence had descended; only the old elm quivered and rustled in the breeze, and any unpleasant thoughts still lingering in her mind now faded as she fixed her gaze more and more closely and with growing enchantment upon the picture spread out

---

* Full proverb: *Si jeunesse savait, si vieillesse pouvait.*

before her. The water streamed softly by, the woods and meadows were bathed in the evening twilight, and the new moon, showing the first sliver of a crescent, cast a gleam of light over the river and picked out its rippling wavelets.

'How lovely,' said Lene with a sigh. 'And I *am* happy,' she added.

She was reluctant to avert her eyes from this picture. But at last she stood up, pushed a chair in front of the mirror, and began to take down her beautiful hair and braid it up again. While she was doing this Botho came in.

'Lene, still up! I thought I'd have to wake you with a kiss.'

'You're too early for that, late as you are.'

And she rose and went towards him. 'My own darling Botho. How long you've been . . .'

'And your temperature? Do you still feel weak?'

'It's passed, and I'm fine now – have been for the past half-hour. And I've been waiting for you all that time.' And she drew him over to the still-open window. 'Just look! How could such a sight not fill a poor human heart with longing?'

She nestled against him and then, closing her eyes, raised her face to his with an expression of purest rapture.

13

THEY WERE BOTH up early, and the sun was still battling its way through the morning mist as they descended the narrow stairs to take breakfast on the ground floor. There was a slight wind, an early morning breeze such as boatmen always like to make use of, and so just as our young couple stepped outside a whole flotilla of Spree flatboats glided past in front of them.

Lene was still wearing her morning robe. She took Botho's arm and strolled with him along a part of the river bank tall with reeds and bulrushes. He looked at her tenderly. 'Lene,

I've never seen you looking like you do now. How can I put it? You look so happy – I can't find another way of saying it.'

And so it was. Yes, she was happy, utterly happy, and saw the whole world in a rosy light. She had the best, the dearest of men on her arm and was enjoying a precious moment with him. Was that not enough? And if this moment should be their last, well, so be it. Was she not favoured just to live through such a day? Even if it was only this once, this one single time?

And so they melted away, all the intimations of hurt and anxiety that despite her best efforts had hitherto oppressed her spirits, and all she felt was pride, joy and thankfulness. But she said nothing; she was too superstitious to tempt fate by speaking of her happiness, and it was only a slight trembling of her arm that made Botho realize how deeply his words had penetrated her heart.

The landlord came over and enquired courteously, albeit with a hint of embarrassment, if they had slept well.

'Splendidly,' said Botho. 'The mint tea that your dear wife prescribed worked wonders, and with the crescent moon shining in through the window and the nightingales singing softly – so softly we could only just hear them – why, who wouldn't sleep as soundly as in paradise itself? I only hope there isn't a Spree steamer with 240 visitors due to arrive this afternoon. That really would expel us from our paradise, without a doubt. You're smiling and probably thinking "Who can tell?", and maybe I'm speaking of the devil. But there's no sign yet, I can't see any funnels or trails of smoke, and the Spree is still perfectly clear, so even if all Berlin is already on its way at least we can eat our breakfast in peace, can't we? But where should we take it?'

'Wherever you'd like to, sir.'

'Well, in that case under the elm, I think. Inside, very nice though it is, only really answers when there's a scorching sun outside. But it's not scorching yet, and over by the woods it still hasn't cleared the mist.'

The landlord went to order their breakfast while the young couple continued their walk along the bank as far as a spit of land, from which they could make out the red roofs of a neighbouring village and, a little to the right, the spire of Königswusterhausen Church. On one side of the spit lay a washed-up willow trunk. They sat on it and watched a fisherman and his wife cutting down the reeds that grew all around and tossing large bundles into their punt. It was a charming picture, and they feasted their eyes on it for a while before returning to the inn, where their breakfast was just being served. This was more in the English than the German style: coffee and tea together with eggs and meat, and even rounds of toasted white bread in a silver rack.

'Well Lene, look at this! We must eat breakfast here more often. What do you think? Divine! And look over there at the boatyard; they're busy caulking again already, working to a proper beat. I honestly believe the rhythmic beat of people at work is the finest music there is.'

Lene nodded, but was only half-listening, for her attention was again fixed on the landing-stage, not this time on the chained-up boats that had so appealed to her the day before, but on a pretty servant girl kneeling in the middle of the boarded walkway next to a pile of copper kitchenware. With a zestful devotion to her task that expressed itself in every movement of her arms she scoured the pots, kettles and pans, and once each item was thoroughly clean she rinsed it in the babbling water. Then she would lift it above her head, so that it sparkled for an instant in the sun, and placed it in a basket at her side.

Lene appeared entranced by the scene. 'Just look,' and she pointed to the pretty girl, who was attacking her work with seemingly limitless gusto.

'You know, Botho, her kneeling there is no coincidence. It's for me she's kneeling, and I can clearly sense providence trying to tell me something.'

'What on earth's the matter, Lene? You've come over quite strange, and you're so pale all of a sudden.'

'It's nothing.'

'Nothing? And yet your eyes are glistening as if you were closer to tears than laughter. Surely it's not the first time you've seen copper pots and pans or a cook scouring them. It's almost as if you envied the girl kneeling there and working fit for three.'

At this point the appearance of the landlord interrupted their conversation, and Lene recovered her composure and soon her cheerfulness too. Then she went upstairs to change.

When she came back down she found that a programme devised by the landlord had been adopted unreservedly by Botho: a sailing boat was to take the young couple to the next village, Niederlehme, charmingly situated on the Wendish Spree, and they would continue on foot to Königswusterhausen, visit the park and the royal hunting lodge there, and then return by the same route. It was a half-day's excursion, and they could decide what to do with the afternoon later on.

Lene agreed with this plan, and a boat was quickly made ready for them. Then, just as a couple of blankets were being carried aboard, they heard voices and hearty laughter coming from the garden, indicating the arrival of other visitors and the prospect that their solitude was about to be disturbed.

'Ah, yachtsmen and rowing club people,' said Botho. 'Thank God we're about to escape them, Lene. Let's hurry up.'

They stood up and made for the boat with all haste. But before they had even reached the landing-stage they found themselves surrounded and trapped. It was Botho's comrades-in-arms, indeed his most intimate circle: Pitt, Serge and Balafré – all three with their ladies. '*Ah, les beaux esprits se rencontrent!*' said Balafré with an exuberance that was nonetheless quickly toned down when he realized that the landlord and landlady were watching him from the threshold of the inn. 'What a piece of luck that we should meet here. Permit me, Gaston, to introduce our ladies: Queen Isabeau, Miss Joan and Miss Margot.'

Botho picked up their chosen code,[*] and, instantly adjusting himself, reciprocated by introducing Lene with a slight wave of the hand: 'Mademoiselle Agnès Sorel'.

The three gentlemen bowed politely, indeed to all appearances respectfully, while the two daughters of Thibault d'Arc, to whom Agnès Sorel was unknown and clearly uncongenial, made exceedingly abrupt curtseys and left it to Queen Isabeau, at least fifteen years their senior, to extend a friendlier greeting.

The whole thing was an intrusion – possibly a planned one – but the greater the likelihood of its being intentional, the more essential it was to grin and bear it. And in this Botho succeeded perfectly. He asked question upon question and learnt that they had made an early start, taking one of the smaller Spree steamers as far as Schmöckwitz and then a sailing boat from there to Zeuthen. From Zeuthen they'd walked the rest of the way, which hadn't even taken twenty minutes. It had been delightful, they said – ancient trees, meadows and red roofs.

While the new arrivals were providing this information, especially the well-upholstered Queen Isabeau, who was almost more remarkable for her powers of speech than for her upholstery, they all wandered over to the veranda and sat at one of the long tables.

'Exquisite!' said Serge. 'Such a free, wide open space and yet so secluded. And that meadow over there is just made for

---

[*] Friedrich Schiller's tragedy *Die Jungfrau von Orleans* (*The Maid of Orleans*, 1801). Margot is Joan of Arc's sister, Queen Isabeau the mother of Charles VII of France, and Agnès Sorel his mistress.

a moonlight stroll.'

'Yes,' Balafré chimed in, 'a moonlight stroll. How very fine. But it's still only ten o'clock in the morning, which gives us a good twelve hours to dispose of before we can have our moonlight stroll. I propose a boating party.'

'No,' said Isabeau, 'no more boating! We've already had our fill of that today. First the steamer, then a sailing boat, and now another one; it's too much. I'm dead against it. I can't see any point in all this plashing around anyway. Next thing you'll want us to go fishing or catch bleaks with our hands and then marvel at the nasty little things. No, we'll have no more plashing around today, if you please!'

The gentlemen, to whom these words were addressed, were visibly amused by the Queen Mother's determination and promptly made alternative suggestions, which, however, met with the same fate. Isabeau rejected everything, and when at last her behaviour began to provoke half-jocular, half-earnest expressions of disapproval she asked for silence: 'Patience, gentlemen! Would you please let me speak for just a moment?' This elicited ironic applause, for so far *she* had done all the talking, but without paying any attention she pressed on: 'Gentlemen, please, I don't need any lessons in gentlemen's tastes. What's a day in the country all about? It's about eating a meal and having a game of cards. Am I right?'

'Isabeau's always right,' said Balafré with a laugh and clapped her on the shoulder. 'We'll have a game of cards. It's a capital spot for it, and almost hard to imagine anyone could lose. Meanwhile the ladies can go for a stroll or have a late-morning nap. That's supposed to do you a world of good, and an hour and a half ought to be enough. Then at twelve we'll join forces. The lunch menu to be left at our Queen's discretion. "Yes, my Queen, 'tis yet sweet to be alive." From *Don Carlos*, admittedly, but does everything have to come from *The Maid*?'

This met with general approval, and the two younger

women giggled at the last word despite not understanding the reference. However Isabeau, who had been exposed to such suggestive and innuendo-filled speech since she was a girl, retained a completely dignified countenance and, turning to the other three women, said: 'Ladies, if you please. We're now dismissed and have two hours to ourselves. Not the worst of prospects, I would say.'

Thereupon they rose from their seats and walked over to the house, where the Queen stepped into the kitchen and with a friendly greeting, though in a superior tone, asked to see the landlord. He was not there, and his young wife said she would call him in from the garden, but Isabeau declined the offer and declared she would go and find him herself, which she then did with her three ladies-in-waiting in tow (a hen and her chicks, Balafré called them). They found the landlord in the garden laying out some new asparagus beds. Just to one side was an old-fashioned hothouse, very low at the front, with large sloping glass panes supported by some rather dilapidated brickwork, on which Lene and the d'Arc girls sat while Isabeau took charge of the negotiations.

'Landlord, we've come to speak to you about lunch. What have you got?'

'Anything the ladies and gentlemen would like to order.'

'Anything? That's a lot, almost too much. In that case I'll go for eel. Not like this, though . . . like this,' she said, pointing first to the ring on her finger and then the bulky, tight-fitting bracelet on her arm.

'I'm sorry, ladies,' replied the landlord. 'We haven't got eel, or any other fish. That's the one thing I can't oblige you with. Yesterday we had tench with dill, but that came from Berlin. If I wanted fish I'd have to go to the Cölln fish market for it.'

'Pity. We could have brought one with us. What else is there?'

'A saddle of venison?'

'Mmm, sounds good. And first a vegetable salad. It's already a bit late for asparagus, or almost, but I can see you've got some young beans there. And you'll no doubt be able to find something here in the hotbed, a few cucumbers or some lamb's lettuce. And then a dessert – something with whipped cream. I could be without it personally, but the gentlemen do love dessert, though they always act as if they didn't care for it. Makes three or four courses, I think. And then bread and butter with cheese.'

'And when would you like it served, madam?'

'Well, soon, I think, or at least as soon as possible. Is that all right? We're pretty hungry, and the venison doesn't need more than half an hour's roasting, so let's say at twelve. And, if I may, a cold punch to go with it: one bottle of Rhine wine, three Moselle and three champagne. But a good label, mind. Believe me, it won't be wasted. I'm perfectly well able to tell the difference between a Moët and a Mumm. But I know you'll do it right. You inspire confidence in me, I must say. By the way, can we get straight from your garden into the woods? I do hate unnecessary walking. Perhaps we'll find some mushrooms. That would be heavenly, and we could have them with the venison. Mushrooms go with everything.'

The landlord not only replied affirmatively to the question about the more convenient path, but escorted the ladies in person as far as the garden gate, from which they were only a few paces from the edge of the woods. Once they had crossed a macadamized road they were already in the shade of the trees, and Isabeau, who was suffering not a little from the ever-increasing heat, counted herself fortunate to have avoided the relatively circuitous route over a stretch of treeless grassland. She closed up her elegant but prominently grease-marked parasol, hung it from her belt, and took Lene's arm, while the other two women followed on behind. Isabeau, evidently in excellent humour, turned back to Margot and Joan and said, 'But we need somewhere to aim for. Just woods and then more woods would be awful. What do you think, Joan?'

Joan was the taller of the two d'Arcs, very pretty, rather pale, and dressed with stylish simplicity. Serge was very particular about this. Her gloves fitted beautifully, and one might have taken her for a lady had she not, while Isabeau was speaking to the landlord, used her teeth to fasten a glove button that had popped open.

'What do you think, Joan?' the Queen repeated her question.

'Well, I suggest we go back to the village we've come from. It was called Zeuthen, I think, and it looked so romantic and so melancholy, it was such a pretty walk from there to here. And it must be just as pretty going the other way, or maybe even prettier. And on the right – or on the left from this side – there was a cemetery with lots of crosses, including a great big marble one.'

'Yes, Joan, my dear, that's all very well, but what's the point? We've already done that walk. Or is it the cemetery … ?'

'Course it is. I can't help my feelings, especially on a day like this. And it's always good to remember that we're all mortal. And now that the lilac's in bloom …'

'But Joan, the lilac's not in bloom any more. Some of the laburnum might still be, but even that's got pods by now. Good Lord, if you're so keen on cemeteries there's one in the Oranienstrasse you can look at every day. But I know it's no use talkin' to you. Zeuthen and cemeteries – what nonsense! We'd be better off stayin' here and not lookin' at anything. Come along, little one, give me your arm again.'

The 'little one', who was not little at all, was Lene. She obeyed, and as they walked on ahead the Queen continued in a confidential tone, 'Honestly, that Joan! You can't take her anywhere; she hasn't got a good name and she's a complete goose. Ah, my pet, you wouldn't believe the sorts you get nowadays. I'm not saying she's not got a good figure, and she takes good care of her gloves. But there's somethin' else she should take care of instead. And you know, it's types like her that are always talkin' about death and cemeteries. You should see her later on, though! She can only keep it up for so long. Once the punchbowl's done the rounds and been filled up again she'll be squealin' and yellin'. No idea of decency. But where should she get that? She was always in low-grade places, out on the main road to Tegel, where hardly anyone ever goes except the odd passing artillery company. And artillery ... well ... you wouldn't believe what a mixed crowd that can be. And now Serge has plucked her out of it and wants to make somethin' of her. Goodness me, it's not that simple, and it'll certainly take time; Rome wasn't built in a day. But look, there's some strawberries. Well, that's a bit of luck. Come on, little one, let's pick some (shame about all the damned bendin' down!), and if we find a really big one we'll take it with us. Then I'll pop it in his mouth, and that'll tickle him. I have to tell you, he's just like a child, that man–he's one of the best.'

Lene could see that she was referring to Balafré and asked some questions, among others her previous one about the strange names the men used. She said she'd asked about it earlier but never got a proper answer.

'Lord,' said the Queen, 'it's supposed to mean somethin', some secret, but it's all just showing off. First of all no one's bothered anyway, and even if they were–what difference would it make? What's the point? There's no harm done, is there? None of them's got anythin' to feel ashamed of, and one's much the same as another.'

Lene looked ahead and said nothing.

'And you'll see for yourself, my pet, it's all quite boring really. It's all right for a bit, and I'm not sayin' anything against it or dissociatin' myself, but you get fed up with it in the long run. Startin' at fifteen, before you're even confirmed. Honestly, the sooner you're out of it again the better. I'm goin' to buy myself a gin-shop (I'll get the money all right), and I know just where; and then I'll marry a widower, and I know which one. And he wants to as well. Because I have to tell you, I'm all for order and decency, and bringin' children up properly, and whether they're his or mine makes no odds at all ... But how are things with you then?'

Lene did not say a word.

'Lord, you're colourin' up, my pet. It hasn't touched you *here*, has it,' and she pointed to her heart, 'and you're doin' it all for love? Well, my pet, then things *are* bad, and there'll be no end of a mess.'

Joan of Arc followed with Margot. They deliberately hung back a little and snapped off some birch twigs as if they intended to weave a garland with them. 'What do you think of her then?' said Margot. 'Gaston's girl, I mean.'

'Think of her? Not much. It really is the limit when ones like that start joinin' in and comin' into fashion! Jus' look at the fit of those gloves. An' her hat's not much better. He really shouldn't let her go about like that. And she must be a bit dim too; she hasn't said a thing.'

'No, she's not dim,' said Margot, 'she jus' hasn't got the hang of it yet. I'd say it's quite clever of her makin' up to our fat friend so fast.'

'Bah, our fat friend! Don't come at me with that! She thinks she's *it*, but she's nothin' special at all. I won't say a word against her otherwise, but she's treacherous, like a snake in the grass.'

'Now that's jus' not true, Joan. What's more she's got you out of hot water many a time. You know very well what I mean.'

'But why, for God's sake? 'cos she was in it herself too, and 'cos she's always puttin' on airs an' actin' important. Fat people like her are never kind.'

'Lord, Joan, the things you say! It's the other way round.

It's the fat ones who *are* kind.'

'Well, have it your own way. But you can't deny that she's a ridiculous sight. Jus' look at the way she's waddlin' along, like an overfed duck. An' always buttoned up to her chin, 'cos otherwise she daren't even show herself among respectable folk. And Margot, don't try and tell me that a reasonably slim figure isn't what really counts. We're not Turks, are we? And why didn't she want to go to the cemetery. 'cos she's afraid? Hardly – wouldn't occur to her. It's 'cos she's all trussed up again and can't take the heat. An' it's not even all that terribly hot today.'

Thus the conversations went on for quite a while before the two pairs reassembled and sat down on the mossy bank of a ditch.

Isabeau kept looking at her watch, but the hands hardly seemed to budge.

When it finally got to half past eleven she said, 'Well, ladies, it's time. I think we've had about enough of the beauties of nature now, and can quite properly move on to somethin' else. Nothing's passed our lips since seven this mornin', because you can't count the ham sandwich at Grünau … But, thank goodness, self-denial brings its own reward, as Balafré says, and hunger's the best sauce. Come along, ladies, that saddle of venison's the main thing now. Don't you think, Joan?'

Joan merely shrugged her shoulders, firmly rejecting the imputation that such things as venison and punch could ever carry any weight with her.

Isabeau laughed, 'Well, we'll see, Joan. The Zeuthen cemetery would've been better, of course, but you have to make do with what you've got.'

And with that they all set off and headed back out of the woods to the garden, in which a few brimstone butterflies were chasing one another, and from there to the front of the inn, where they were to have lunch.

Passing the restaurant Isabeau caught a glimpse of the landlord upending a bottle of Moselle wine.

'A pity,' she said, 'that *that* is what I had to see. I think fate might have granted me a pleasanter sight. Why did it have to be Moselle?'

14

DESPITE Isabeau's best exertions it had proved impossible, after this walk, to restore any real gaiety to the party. Even worse, at least for Botho and Lene, was that gaiety remained absent even when they had said goodbye to Botho's friends and their ladies and were sitting in a compartment all to themselves on the return journey. An hour later they had arrived, low in spirits, under the dreary lamplight of Görlitz Station, and as soon as they alighted Lene had asked with something akin to urgency that she be left to make her own way through the city. It was for the best, she said, as they were tired and out of sorts, but Botho was not to be deflected from what he saw as his gentlemanly duty to show her the proper attentions, and so together they had taken a rickety old cab for the long, long drive beside the canal, trying throughout to get up a conversation about the excursion and how lovely it had been – a horribly forced exchange that had made Botho feel only too strongly how right Lene's instinct had been in more or less imploring him not to accompany her. The truth was that the trip to Hankel's Stowage, on which they had embarked with such eager anticipation and which had indeed begun so beautifully and happily, had ended in nothing but ill-humour, weariness and enervation. Only at the final moment, when Botho had said his 'Goodnight, Lene' with a loving warmth and a certain sense of guilt, had she rushed back to him and, seizing his hand, kissed him with an almost impetuous passion: 'Oh, Botho, today wasn't how it should have been, but no one was to blame ... Not even the others.'

'Don't, Lene.'

'No, no. No one was to blame, that's the truth, and we can't change it. But that's what makes it so bad. If someone's to blame they can ask for forgiveness and all's well again. But that's no help to us. In any case there's nothing to forgive.'

'Lene ...'

'Do listen to me. Oh, my own precious Botho, you're trying to hide it from me, but it's all coming to an end. And quickly, I know it is.'

'What are you saying?'

'I admit it was only something I dreamt,' Lene continued. 'But why would I dream it? Because it was preoccupying me the whole day. My dream was just what I was turning over in my heart. But the other thing I wanted to say to you, Botho, the reason I ran these few steps after you, is that I still stand by what I said to you last night. Life through this summer has been a joy to me, a joy that can't be taken away, even if I'm unhappy from this day onwards.'

'Lene, Lene, don't talk like this ...'

'You can sense that I'm right yourself; it's just that your kind heart refuses to accept it, and doesn't want to admit it. But I know. Yesterday, when we walked through the meadow together chatting and I picked you the posy, that was our last real happiness and our last precious moment.'

The day had ended with this conversation, and now the next morning had come and the summer sun was shining brightly into Botho's room. Both windows stood open, and sparrows were chirping in the chestnut trees outside. Botho was leaning back in his rocking chair smoking a meerschaum pipe, occasionally flicking the handkerchief lying next to him at a large blowfly which, as soon as it had gone out of one window, immediately reappeared at the other and then continued to buzz obstinately and relentlessly around him.

'If only I could get rid of the pest! I'd like to make it really squirm with pain. These blowflies are always bringers of bad tidings, and seem to take malicious pleasure in the troubles whose heralds and prophets they are.' Once more he struck out at it. 'Got away again. It's no use. May as well resign myself. Submission is always the best policy. The Turks[*] have got the right idea.'

The sound of the little iron gate outside being banged shut made him look across the front garden during his soliloquy and see the postman arrive. A moment later, with a brief salute and a 'Good morning, Herr Baron', he handed him a newspaper and then a letter through the relatively low ground-floor window. Botho threw the newspaper aside and scanned the letter, on which he had easily recognized the small, close and yet clearly legible handwriting of his mother. 'I thought as much ... I know what it says without even looking. Poor Lene.'

Then he opened the letter and read:

Zehden Manor, 29th June 1875

My dear Botho,

The apprehension I communicated to you in my last letter has now become a reality: Rothmüller in Arnswalde has given notice of foreclosing from 1st October while saying that if this created difficulties for me he would be prepared, 'as an old family friend', to wait until the New Year. He was, as he added, very mindful of the respect he owed to the late baron's memory. This last remark, which may have been perfectly well meant, is doubly painful to me: it contains so much pretentious solicitude, which it

---

[*] Allusion to the notion that Turks and other Muslims are resigned to what they see as their *kismet*.

is never pleasant to experience, and least of all from that quarter. You can perhaps understand the vexation and worry his letter has caused me. Uncle Kurt Anton would help as on earlier occasions, for he is very fond of me and above all of *you*, but it weighs on me terribly to make such repeated claims on his affection, not least as he puts the blame for our endless difficulties on our whole family, but especially on you and me. Although I honestly strive after economy in running the estate he does not find me economical enough or modest enough in my needs, and he may well be right. As for you, he does not consider you sufficiently practical and worldly-wise, and here too he has probably hit the mark. Well, Botho, you see how things are. My brother possesses a very fine sense of what is fair and reasonable, and a truly exceptional *gentilezza* in money matters (something that cannot be said for many of the families of quality in these parts, for of all provinces our dear old Mark Brandenburg is the thriftiest, and, where a helping hand is needed, the most squeamish). And yet, generous as he is, he does have his little whims and vagaries, and being persistently crossed in these has put him out of all humour for quite a while now. The other day, when I took the opportunity of mentioning the renewed threat of foreclosure hanging over us, he said, 'I'm glad to be of service, as you know, my dear sister, but I must frankly confess that always having to help where, with a bit more judgement and a bit less stubbornness, one could at a stroke help oneself makes rather a heavy demand on one of my least well-developed qualities – my indulgence, that is . . .' You know what this refers to, Botho, and I now urge *you* to take his words to heart, just as Uncle Kurt Anton clearly wanted *me* to take them to heart. To judge from things you have said and from your letters, there is nothing you abominate more than sentimentality, and yet I fear that you are yourself caught up in it, more

deeply than you care to admit or maybe even realize. I shall
say no more.

Rienäcker put the letter aside and paced up and down the
room, half-mechanically exchanging his meerschaum for a
cigarette as he did so. Then he took the letter up again and
read on.

Yes, Botho, you hold the family's future in your hands and
must determine whether this feeling of constant depend-
ency is to continue or not. But when I say you hold it in
your hands, I am obliged to add: only for a short time,
at any rate not for very much longer. Uncle Kurt Anton
has spoken to me of this too, I mean regarding Frau
von Sellenthin, who during his last visit to Rothenmoor
expressed herself very decidedly and even with some irri-
tability on this topic, which concerns her greatly. She
asked if the Rienäcker family perhaps believe that, like
the Sibylline Books, a fortune becomes more valuable as it
gets smaller (where she got that comparison from I do not
know). Käthe is now nearly twenty-two, she said, with all
the polish of good society, and thanks to the legacy from
her Kielmannsegge aunt disposes of a fortune on which
the interest probably amounts to very little less than the
capital value of the Rienäcker heathland, whitefish lake
included. One does not keep a young lady in her position
waiting, she said, least of all with such persistence and
equanimity. If it pleases Herr von Rienäcker to drop what
has earlier been planned and arranged by his family, and
regard the engagements entered into as mere bagatelles,
she will make no objection. Herr von Rienäcker can be free
the moment he wishes to be free. If, on the other hand, he
does not propose to make use of this unconditional right to
withdraw, it is time to make this plain. She does not wish
her daughter to become the subject of idle talk.

You will readily gather from the tone of this that it is imperative to come to a decision and act on it. You know what I wish. However, my wishes should not bind you. Decide one way or the other and act as your own good sense directs you, but do act! Withdrawal is more honourable than further procrastination. If you hesitate any longer we lose not just the bride, but the goodwill of the whole Sellenthin family, and, even worse, indeed worst of all, your uncle's affectionate sentiments and constant willingness to help. My thoughts are with you – may they also guide you. I repeat: it would be the path to happiness for you and for us all. And with that I remain

Ever your loving mother Josephine von R.

By the time he had finished reading Botho was greatly agitated. The situation was as the letter described it, and further postponement impossible. The Rienäcker fortune was in a bad way, and he keenly sensed that he lacked the willpower, shrewdness and energy required to overcome the prevailing difficulties.

'What am I? A completely ordinary person from the so-called higher reaches of society. And what can I do? I can train a horse, carve a capon, and play games of chance. That's all, and so my choice is between circus rider, head waiter and croupier. Or at a pinch a trooper if I decide to join a foreign legion. And Lene could come with me as a daughter of the regiment. I can just see her in a short skirt and high-heeled boots with a little keg strapped to her back.'[*]

He continued in this vein and indulged in some bitter self-criticism. At last he rang the bell and ordered that his horse be made ready as he wished to ride out. Before long his splendid chestnut mare, a gift from his uncle and the envy of

---

[*] The canteen-girl heroine of Donizetti's comic opera *La Fille du régiment* wears such a costume.

his fellow officers, was standing outside. He swung himself into the saddle, gave his batman a few instructions, and then rode towards Moabit Bridge, which he then crossed before turning onto a broad path that led across some marshland and fields to Jungfern Heath. Here he let his horse drop from a trot to a walk and turned his mind, hitherto immersed in all sorts of vague musings, to an ever more rigorous and pointed self-interrogation. 'So what's preventing me from taking the step that everyone expects of me? Do I mean to marry Lene? No. Have I promised her I would? No. Does she expect it? No. Or will parting be any easier for us if I defer it? No, no, and no again. And yet I hesitate and vacillate instead of doing the *one* thing I most certainly must do. And why do I hesitate? Why this vacillation and postponement? Foolish question! Because I love her.'

The sound of artillery fire from the Tegel range inter-rupted him at this point and momentarily unsettled his horse. Once he had quieted it he took up his train of thought again and repeated, 'Because I love her! Yes. And why should I be ashamed of this attachment? Our feelings recognize no laws, and the fact of loving someone is its own justification, however much everyone else might shake their heads or call it a mystery. In any case it isn't a mystery, or if it is I can easily solve it. Each person is predisposed by nature towards certain things, sometimes very, very small in themselves, but although small they are the stuff of life to that person or at least the best that life has to offer. And for me these things are simplicity, truth and naturalness. Lene has them all, that's been her fascination for me, there lies the magical spell that I find so hard to break.'

Just then his horse shied, and he caught sight of a startled hare darting out of a strip of meadow and racing directly in front of him towards Jungfern Heath. He followed it curi-ously with his eyes and only returned to his reflections once the fleeing animal had disappeared into the undergrowth of the heath. 'And was what I wished for so foolish and unthinkable? No. It isn't in me to challenge the world and openly declare war on it and its prejudices. I'm completely against that kind of tilting at windmills. All I wanted was a happiness hidden from view, a happiness for which I sooner or later anticipated society's tacit approval in return for not having outraged its conventions. That was my dream, the substance of my thoughts and hopes. And now I'm to give up this happiness in exchange for something that won't make me happy at all. Drawing-room society leaves me cold and I have an aversion to everything that's inauthentic and artificially concocted, *chic, tournure, savoir-faire* – words as ugly to my ears as they are foreign.'

At this point his horse, which for a quarter of an hour had enjoyed a very slack rein, turned as if of its own volition into a side-path that led first to a piece of tilled land and beyond it to a patch of grass enclosed by undergrowth and a few oaks. Here, in the shade of one of the older trees, stood a small, squat stone cross, and on approaching to see what this cross signified Botho saw the words *Ludwig von Hinckeldey,*[*] *died 10th March 1856*. What a jolt it gave him! He had known that the cross was located hereabouts, but had never come this far before, and now he thought it must be a sign that his horse had brought him unbidden to this very spot.

Hinckeldey! It was getting on for twenty years since the then all-powerful man had met his end, and all the discussions the news had provoked in his parents' home came flooding back into his mind. He recalled one story especially. One of the police chief's most trusted lieutenants, a man of middle-class stock, had warned and urged him to hold back,

---

[*] General director of police under Frederick William IV. His decision to close an aristocratic gambling club prompted a public insult from one of its members. Forced by the code of honour to demand satisfaction, Hinckeldey was shot dead in the ensuing duel.

describing duels in general, and this one in particular, given the circumstances attending it, as criminal nonsense. But his superior, choosing *this* moment for an unwonted display of his noble credentials, gave the abrupt and haughty reply, 'Nörner, these are things you don't understand.' And one hour later he went to his death. And for what? For the sake of an aristocratic notion, a class whim that was stronger than all his powers of reason, stronger even than the law which he more than anyone had a duty to uphold and defend. 'Instructive. And what can I personally learn from this? What moral does this monument teach *me*? One thing at any rate: that background determines conduct. A man who goes with the grain may fall, but he falls in a better way than a man who goes against it.'

While he was pondering this he turned his horse around and rode across country towards a large factory, a rolling mill or engineering works, from the numerous chimneys of which dense smoke and fiery columns rose into the air. It was midday, and some of the workers were sitting outside in the shade eating their meal. Their wives, who had brought the food, stood to one side chatting, some nursing babies in their arms, and turned laughing faces to one another whenever a roguish or teasing remark was directed at them. Rienäcker, whose claim to have a liking for naturalness was only too well founded, was enchanted by the picture that the happy group presented to him, and watched with a touch of envy. 'Work and daily bread and order. When our natives of the Mark marry, they don't speak of passion or love; they simply say, "I must put everything in order." And that's an admirable feature of our people, not humdrum at all. Because order means a lot – everything sometimes. And now I ask myself, has there been "order" in my life? No. Order is marriage.' After he had soliloquized a little longer in this strain he again saw Lene standing before him, and in her eyes there was no hint of reproach or accusation; on the contrary, it was as if she were gently nodding her assent.

'Yes, my darling Lene, work and order are your principles too, and you can see how things are and won't make it hard for me ... But it is hard all the same ... for you and for me.'

He raised his horse back to a trot and covered a stretch close by the Spree. When he reached the pavilion restaurant In den Zelten, calm in the midday lull, he turned onto a bridle path that led him to the Wrangel Fountain and soon after to his own door.

15

BOTHO intended to go straight to Lene, but feeling he lacked the strength to do so he intended at least to write. But even that was too much. 'I can't, not today.' And so he let the day go by and waited until the next morning. Then he wrote a short note:

My dear Lene!

What you predicted the day before yesterday has now come true. We must part. And for ever. I've had letters from home that force my hand. It must be, and so let it be quick ... Oh, how I wish these days lay behind us! I'll say no more to you now, not even how I feel ... It was a brief but beautiful time, and I won't forget a moment of it. I'll be with you about nine – not before because it mustn't last long. Goodbye, for the second last time goodbye.

Your B. v. R.

And now he came. Lene stood at the gate and received him as she usually did; there was not the smallest trace of reproach or even painful resignation in her face. She took his arm and they walked along the front-garden path.

'You were right to come ... I'm glad you're here. And I hope you're glad too.'

As she spoke they reached the house, and Botho made as if to step from the hallway into the large front room as usual. But Lene drew him away, saying, 'No, Frau Dörr's in there ...'

'Is she still angry with us?'

'No, no. I've calmed her down. But what do we want with her today? Come on, it's such a lovely evening, and we want to be alone.'

He agreed, and they passed through the hallway and across the yard towards the garden. Sultan did not stir, merely blinking at them as they walked up the broad middle path and then over to the bench between the raspberry bushes.

There they sat down. Other than some chirping coming from the fields all was quiet, and the moon stood above them.

She leant against him and said quietly and fondly, 'So this is the last time I'll hold your hand in mine?'

'Yes, Lene. Can you forgive me?'

'What questions you ask. What's there to forgive?'

'That I've made your heart ache.'

'Yes, it does ache. That's true.'

And then she was silent again and looked up at the pale stars filling the sky.

'What are you thinking, Lene?'

'How nice it would be to be up there.'

'Don't talk like that. You mustn't wish your life away; from such a wish it's only a step ...'

She smiled. 'No, I don't mean that. I'm not like the girl who ran to the well and threw herself in because her sweetheart danced with someone else. Do you remember telling me about her?'

'Why mention it then? It's not like you to say something like that just for the sake of saying something.'

'No, I did mean it seriously. And really,' she said pointing upwards, 'I'd like to be there. Then I'd be at peace. But I can wait ... Come on, let's go for a walk in the fields. I haven't brought my shawl out with me and I'm getting cold just sitting still.'

And so they walked along the same field path that on the earlier occasion had taken them as far as the first row of houses in Wilmersdorf. Its steeple was clearly visible under the bright, starry sky, and only the meadow wore a thin veil of mist.

'Do you remember,' said Botho, 'when we came this way with Frau Dörr?'

She nodded. 'That's why I suggested it. I wasn't really cold at all, or hardly. Ah, what a beautiful day it was, and I've never been so cheerful and happy, not before or since. Even now my heart leaps at the thought of how we walked along singing *Do you still remember*? Yes, memories mean so much – everything. I've got memories that will stay with me and no one can ever take away. And that makes me feel so much better.'

He embraced her. 'How good you are!'

But Lene went on talking in her tranquil voice, 'And I don't want to let this feeling pass without telling you everything I have to say. It's really just what I've told you all along, and again the day before yesterday on our half-spoiled excursion and then later when we said goodbye. I've seen this coming, seen it from the start, and what's happened is what was bound to happen. If you've had a beautiful dream you should thank God for it and not complain when the dream ends and reality returns. At this moment it's hard, but everything will probably be forgotten or at least appear in a more positive light. And one day you'll be happy again and maybe I shall too.'

'Do you think so? And if not, what then?'

'Then life goes on without happiness.'

'Oh, Lene, you say that so easily as if happiness didn't matter. But it does, and that's what's troubling me. I feel as if I've wronged you.'

'I'll never accuse you of that. You haven't wronged me, you haven't led me astray, and you haven't made me any promises. It was all my own free choice. I've loved you with all my heart, that was my fate, and if there's any blame in that then it's mine. But it's a blame I rejoice in with my whole being, as I can't tell you often enough, because it made me so happy. If I have to pay for it now I gladly will. You haven't offended me or injured me or insulted me, or if you have then only in terms of what people call morality and respectability. Should I grieve at that? No. Everything will right itself, and that too. Come on, let's turn back. Look how the mist is rising. I think Frau Dörr will have gone by now, and we'll find the dear old soul alone. She knows everything, and all day she's kept on saying the same thing.'

'What's that?'

'That it's for the best.'

Frau Nimptsch was indeed alone when Botho and Lene joined her. Everything was quiet and dusky, and only the fire in the hearth cast a gleam of light over the bulky shadows slanting across the room. The goldfinch had long since gone to sleep in its cage, and nothing could be heard except the occasional hiss of water boiling over.

'Good evening, mother,' said Botho.

The old woman returned his greeting and was about to rise from her footstool and pull up the big armchair. But Botho would not let her, saying, 'No, no, mother, I'll sit in my old place.'

And he pushed the other stool close to the fire.

There was a moment's pause before he started speaking again: 'I've come today to say goodbye and to thank you for all the goodness and kindness I've received here for so long. Yes, mother, I thank you with all my heart. I've so enjoyed coming here and been so happy. But now I must go away, and all I can say is this: it's best this way.'

Silently the old woman nodded in agreement. 'But I shan't be on the other side of the moon,' Botho went on, 'and I won't forget you, mother. And now give me your hand. That's right. Goodnight to you.'

With that he stood up quickly and walked over to the door, with Lene holding onto his arm. They made their way as far as the garden gate without speaking another word. Then she said, 'Quickly now, Botho. I don't have much more strength; it was all too much, these last two days. Farewell, my dearest, and be as happy as you deserve, and as happy as you've made me. Then you will be happy. As for the rest, let's not talk about it any more; it's not important. Hush, hush.'

And she kissed him once, and then again, and then closed the gate.

When he reached the other side of the road and saw Lene again from there, he seemed to want to turn back for one last exchange of words and kisses. But she waved him away vehemently, and so he continued down the road, while she, her head on her arm and her arm on the gatepost, gazed wide-eyed after him.

And she stood there a long while, until the sound of his footsteps died away in the stillness of the night.

16

THE WEDDING took place at the Sellenthin estate of Rothenmoor in mid-September. Uncle Kurt Anton, usually a reluctant public speaker, proposed the health of the bride and groom in what was doubtless the longest toast of his life, and the following day the personal column of the *Kreuzzeitung* carried the following notice: 'Baron Botho von Rienäcker, First Lieutenant, Imperial Cuirassier Regiment, and Baroness Käthe von Rienäcker, *née* von Sellenthin, herewith

respectfully announce their marriage celebrated yesterday.'
Naturally the *Kreuzzeitung* was not a paper that normally
penetrated the Dörrs' market garden, either its main dwelling
or any other part of the domain, but the very next morning
a letter arrived for 'The Honourable Fräulein Magdalene
Nimptsch' containing nothing except a cutting with the
wedding announcement. Lene flinched, but regained her
composure more quickly than the sender, in all probability an
envious fellow-seamstress, might have expected. That it came
from such a quarter could be surmised from the honorific
before her name; however, this taunt, intended as an extra
twist of the knife, served on the contrary to temper the bitter
feeling that this piece of news would otherwise have caused
her.

Before their wedding day was out Botho and Käthe von
Rienäcker started for Dresden, having managed to resist the
temptation to travel to the Neumark for a series of family
visits. Nor did they have any reason to regret their choice,
least of all Botho, who congratulated himself daily on having
come to Dresden, but much more on the possession of his
young wife, who seemed a complete stranger to capricious-
ness and bad moods. Indeed she laughed all day long, and
her nature was as radiant as her features and as fair as her
hair. Everything entertained her and made her laugh. There
was a waiter in the hotel who wore a toupee that looked like
the dipping crest of a wave, and this waiter and his hairpiece
were her daily delight – so much so that, though otherwise
not especially sharp-witted, she hit on an endless stream
of images and comparisons to describe it. Botho shared
her delight and laughed along heartily, until all at once an
element of misgiving and even uneasiness entered his mirth.
For he perceived that she was interested only in the trivial
and comical aspect of whatever she saw or experienced, and
a brief conversation as they set off on their journey back to
Berlin after about a fortnight's happy stay fully confirmed his

impression of this feature of his wife's character. They had a compartment to themselves, and as they crossed the bridge over the Elbe and turned their heads back for a farewell glance at Dresden's Old Town and the dome of the Church of Our Lady, he took her hand and said, 'And now tell me, Käthe, what was the best thing of all here in Dresden?'

'Guess!'

'Well, that's not easy. You've got your own particular taste, and it's no use my suggesting church music or the Holbein Madonna.'

'No, you're right there. But I won't keep my lord and master on tenterhooks a moment longer. There were three things that pleased me most: first and foremost the cake shop on the corner of the Altmarkt and the Scheffelgasse with its wonderful pastries and liqueurs. Just sitting there ...'

'But Käthe, we couldn't sit at all; we could hardly stand, and it felt as if we had to fight for every morsel!'

'That's exactly it. That was the appeal, my dear. Anything you have to fight for ...'

And she turned away and pouted playfully until he gave her a hearty kiss.

'I can see,' she laughed, 'that you've finally come round to my opinion, and as a reward I'll tell you the second and third things. The second was the open-air summer theatre where we saw *Monsieur Herkules*[*] and Knaak drumming the *Tannhäuser* March on a rickety old whist table. I've never seen anything so comical in all my life, and I don't believe you have either. It really was too comical ... And the third ... well, the third was *Bacchus Riding the Billy Goat* in the Grünes Gewölbe Collection and the *Dog Scratching Itself* by Peter Vischer.'

'I thought as much, and if Uncle Kurt Anton hears what you've said he'll agree with you and be fonder of you than

---

[*] A one-act comedy of mistaken identity by Georg Belly (1836-75).

ever and repeat to me even more often: "I'm telling you, Botho, your Käthe ..."'

'Shouldn't he, then?'

'Of course he should.'

With that they broke off for a few minutes, and Botho, even as he looked tenderly and lovingly across at his young wife, yet felt a little troubled as the words they had just exchanged lingered in his mind. She for her part had no inkling of what her husband was thinking, and simply remarked, 'I'm tired, Botho. All those pictures, it's catching up with me ...' Then, as the train came to a stop, 'What's all that noise and commotion outside?'

'It's a pleasure resort for Dresdeners. Kötzschenbroda, I think.'

'Kötzschenbroda? Too comical!'

And as the train steamed onwards again she stretched herself out and appeared to close her eyes. She was not asleep, though, and through her lashes she looked across at her beloved husband.

Meanwhile Käthe's mother had furnished an apartment for them in the Landgrafenstrasse, which at that time was still only built up on one side, and on their return to Berlin at the beginning of October the young couple were enchanted at how comfortable it was. The two front rooms, each with its own fireplace, were heated, but as the autumn air was mild the doors and windows were thrown open and the fires burned only for show and to ventilate the rooms. Finest of all was the large balcony, fully screened from above by a capacious low-hanging awning, beneath which one had a view, first over a small birch wood and the Zoological Gardens, and, beyond that, straight over open country as far as the northernmost point of the Grunewald.

Käthe clapped her hands in delight at this splendidly unimpeded prospect. She embraced her mother and kissed

Botho, and then suddenly pointed to her left, where a shingled steeple could be seen between a few isolated poplars and willows. 'Look, Botho, how comical! It looks as if it's kinked in three places. And the village next to it, what's that called?'

'Wilmersdorf, I think,' stuttered Botho.

'Well then, Wilmersdorf. But why do you say "I think"? Surely you know the names of the villages round here. Just look at the face he's making, Mama, as if he'd given away a state secret. These men really are too comical!'

And with that they withdrew from the balcony into the room to take their first luncheon *en famille*: just Käthe's mother, the young couple, and Serge as the sole guest.

The Rienäckers' apartment was not even a thousand paces from Frau Nimptsch's house. But Lene knew nothing of this and often passed through the Landgrafenstrasse, which she would have avoided had she had even the smallest suspicion of who lived there.

However, it could not remain unknown to her for long.

It was already the third week of October, but still felt like summer, with the sun giving so much warmth that the sharper bite of the air was barely perceptible.

'I have to go into town today, mother,' said Lene. 'Goldstein's written to me. He wants to speak to me about a pattern to be embroidered on the Princess of Waldeck's linen. And while I'm in town I'll go and see Frau Demuth in the Alte Jakobstrasse. It's so easy to fall out of touch with people. But I'll be back by midday. I'll tell Frau Dörr, so that she can look in on you.'

'No need, Lene, no need. I'd rather be on my own. And Frau Dörr, she does go on so, an' always about her husband. Besides, I've got my fire, an' if the goldfinch chirps now and then that's company enough. But if you could bring me a bag of sweets, I've had such a nasty tickle in my throat lately, and those malt lozenges are so soothin'.

'I will, mother.'

Thereupon Lene left the tranquil little house and walked down the Kurfürstenstrasse and then all along the Potsdamerstrasse towards the Spittelmarkt, where the offices of Goldstein Brothers were located. Everything went smoothly, and with midday approaching she made her way home, this time taking the Lützowstrasse instead of the Kurfürstenstrasse. The sun did her good, and she was so entertained by the bustle on the Magdeburger Platz, where the weekly market was just ending and the traders making ready to depart, that she stopped to watch the colourful jumble of activities. For a while it seemed to put her in a trance, from which she was only roused by the din of the fire brigade clattering past.

Lene listened until the jangling and clanging had died away in the distance, and then glanced left down the street at the clock tower of the Church of the Twelve Apostles. 'Twelve exactly. I'd better hurry; she always starts worrying if I come later than she expects.' And so she continued along the Lützowstrasse towards the Lützowplatz. Then suddenly she stopped and did not know where to turn, for a very short distance away she recognized Botho, who was coming straight towards her with a beautiful young lady on his arm. The young lady was speaking with animation, and apparently on amusing topics, for Botho laughed constantly as he looked down at her. It was thanks to this that he had not long ago spotted Lene, who, instantly resolving to avoid a meeting at all costs, turned right on the pavement and stepped up to the nearest large shop window, in front of which lay a square, grooved iron grating, presumably covering the entrance to a cellar. The window itself belonged to an ordinary household goods shop, with the usual display of tallow candles and jars of mixed pickles – nothing special, but Lene stared as if she had never seen the like of it before. She was just in time, for a second later the young couple all but brushed past her, so that not a single word of their exchange escaped her.

'Käthe, not so loud,' Botho was saying, 'people are beginning to stare.'

'Let them ...'

'They'll probably think we're quarrelling.'

'What, and laughing? Quarrelling and laughing?'

And she laughed again.

Lene could feel the thin iron grating tremble beneath her feet. There was a horizontal brass rail across the front of the shop window to protect the large glass pane, and for a second she thought she would have to grasp it for support. However, she managed to hold herself upright, and only when she could be sure that the two of them were far enough away did she turn again and walk on. For a short stretch she was able to pick her way gingerly past the houses, but soon she felt faint, and once she reached the next side-street leading off towards the canal she turned into it and entered a front garden whose gate had been left open. With her last strength she dragged herself to a small flight of steps leading up to the veranda and the raised ground floor and, close to passing out, sat down on one of them.

When she came to again she saw an adolescent girl standing next to her holding a little spade, with which she had dug a few small beds. The girl looked at her sympathetically, while with almost equal curiosity an old nanny was scrutinizing her from the veranda balustrade. It seemed that nobody was at home except the child and the servant, and Lene, apologizing to them both, got up and walked back to the gate. The girl gazed after her in sad wonderment, almost as if a premonition of life's sorrows had just dawned in her childish heart.

Lene had now crossed the embankment and reached the canal, which she walked along, keeping to the foot of the slope where she could be sure of not meeting anyone. From time to time a spitz yelped on one of the barges, and as it was midday thin lines of smoke rose from the cabin stovepipes. But she saw and heard nothing of this, or at any rate was unaware of what was going on around her; and it was not until she had got to the far side of the Zoological Gardens, where the houses lining the canal came to an end and the big sluicegate with water foaming over it came into view, that she stopped and gasped for breath. 'Ah, if only I could cry!' And she pressed her hand against her breast and heart.

Home again she found her mother in her usual place and sat down opposite her, without either of them exchanging a word or a glance. But then the old woman, whose gaze had been riveted on the fire in her hearth, looked up sharply and took fright when she saw the alteration in Lene's features.

'Lene, my child, what's the matter? Lene, you look so strange?' And sluggish as she normally was, she now rose from her footstool in an instant and searched for the jug to sprinkle some water on the girl, who still sat there looking more dead than alive. But the jug was empty, and so she hobbled to the hallway and from there out into the yard and garden to call the good Frau Dörr, who was busy cutting wallflowers and honeysuckle to tie into bunches for market. Her husband was standing beside her, saying 'Don't use so much string this time.'

Frau Dörr turned pale when she heard the old woman's pitiful cries a little way off, and in a loud voice she answered, 'I'm comin', Mother Nimptsch, I'm comin''; and throwing down the flowers and raffia in her hands, she immediately ran over to the little front house, telling herself something must be wrong.

'Yes, jus' as I thought ... Our Lene,' and with that she shook the still lifeless girl vigorously, while the old woman slowly came after her and shuffled across the hallway.

'We've got to get her to bed,' cried Frau Dörr, and Frau Nimptsch made ready to give her a hand. But that was not what the imposing woman had meant by 'we'. 'I'll be better doin' it myself, Mother Nimptsch,' and taking Lene in her arms, she carried her into the small adjoining room and tucked her up.

'There, Mother Nimptsch. And now she wants a hot dish-cover. I can tell what it is – it's the blood. First the dish-cover and then a hot brick to the soles of her feet. Right under the instep, mind, that's where the life is ... But what brought it on? Must be some kind of shock.'

'Don't know. She didn't say a word. But I think maybe she's seen him.'

'Quite right. That's it. I can tell ... And now the windows closed and the blinds down ... Some'd try camphor and Hoffmann's Drops, but camphor saps your strength an' it's only really fit for moths. No, my dear old Nimptsch, with a constitution like hers, young and strong, you're best left to right yourself, so let her sweat it out, I say. A really good sweat, mind. And what's the cause of it all? Men, that's what. And still we need 'em and can't do without ... Aha, she's already gettin' a bit of colour back.'

'Wouldn't we be better off sendin' for a doctor?'

'God forbid! They're all drivin' around on house calls now, and she could go to heaven three times over before you'd get hold of one.'

17

TWO AND A HALF years had elapsed since this encounter, and during that time much had changed in our circle of friends and acquaintances, but not for the residents of the Landgrafenstrasse.

Here the same good humour prevailed, the gaiety of the honeymoon lived on, and Käthe laughed as much as ever. The fact that the couple remained simply a couple, which might have saddened other young wives, did not cause Käthe a moment's pain. She took so much pleasure in life, was so completely satisfied with clothes and chit-chat, riding and driving, that she dreaded rather than wished for a change in her domestic circumstances. No readiness, let alone yearning, for a family of her own had yet awoken in her, and when her mother made a remark on this subject in a letter, Käthe replied in a rather irreverent tone: 'Don't worry, Mama. Botho's brother is also engaged now and the wedding is six months from now, so I shall gladly yield the responsibility for continuing the Rienäcker line to my future sister-in-law.'

Botho saw things differently, but the absence of what might have made his home life complete did not greatly cloud his happiness either, and if he nonetheless had occasional moments of discontent, it was principally, as before on the honeymoon in Dresden, because although he could conduct a passably sensible conversation with Käthe it could never be a serious one. She was entertaining and sometimes brought off a witty observation, but even the best of what she said was superficial and frisky, as if she lacked the ability to distinguish between important and unimportant things. And the worst of it was that she regarded all this as a virtue, took pride in it, and had no notion of giving it up. 'But Käthe, Käthe,' Botho would protest, introducing a trace of disapproval into his voice, but her winsome nature always succeeded in disarming him, so much so that he almost felt pedantic for making such demands of her.

Lene, with her simplicity, truthfulness and lack of empty talk, often came into his mind, but quickly faded again, and only when chance occurrences brought back strikingly vivid memories of particular incidents did he experience stronger feelings and sometimes even uncomfortable moments.

One such occurrence came in the young couple's first summer, as they sat on their balcony drinking tea after returning from a dinner party at Count Alten's. Käthe was leaning back in her chair while Botho read her a newspaper article crammed with figures on the subject of parsonage and surplice fees. She took little of it in, not least because the figures confused her, but she still listened fairly attentively, because all girls of good family from the Mark spend half their childhood 'among the cloth' and later maintain a sympathetic interest in parsonage affairs. And so it was today. At last evening drew in, and just as darkness was falling the band struck up over in the Zoological Gardens, and a charming Strauss waltz lilted across.

'Listen, Botho,' said Käthe, sitting up straight, and then added exuberantly, 'Come on, let's dance.' And without waiting for his consent she pulled him up from his chair and waltzed with him into the large room leading off the balcony and then a few times around it. Then she gave him a kiss and nestled up to him. 'You know, Botho, I've never had such a wonderful dance, not even at my first ball, which was when I was still at Fräulein Zülow's school and, I must confess, not even confirmed. Uncle Kurt Anton took me on his own responsibility, and Mama knows nothing about it to this day. But even that wasn't as lovely as today. And yet forbidden fruit is supposed to taste best, isn't it? But you're not saying anything, you look embarrassed, Botho. See, I've caught you out again!'

He tried his best to frame a reply, but she did not give him a chance: 'I honestly believe, Botho, that you've fallen for my sister Ine, and don't try and reassure me by saying she's still a slip of a girl or not much more. They're always the most dangerous. Isn't that so? Well, I'll pretend I haven't noticed, and I won't hold it against you or her. But I'm jealous about older romances, even from long ago – much, much more jealous than about new ones.'

'How strange,' said Botho, attempting a laugh.

'Not as strange as it might seem,' Käthe continued. 'You see, you can always keep half an eye on new romances, and things have to take a pretty bad turn or there has to be a big deceiver at work for you not to notice anything and be completely fooled. But there's no way of checking up on old romances; there might have been a hundred and one and you'd hardly know.'

'And what you don't know –'

'– can *still* hurt you. But let's drop the subject, and you go on reading to me from your paper instead. I constantly have to think of our friends the Kluckhuhns, and how little grasp the good woman has on things. And their eldest son about to go to university.'

Incidents like this occurred again and again, conjuring up images of old times and of Lene herself in Botho's mind; but he never actually saw her, which struck him as odd as he knew that they were almost neighbours.

It struck him as odd, but he would have found it perfectly natural if he had been told that Frau Nimptsch and Lene had long since quitted their old abode, as indeed they had. From the very day of her encounter with the young couple in the Lützowstrasse, Lene had made it clear that it was impossible for her to continue to live in the house they rented from the Dörrs, and when Frau Nimptsch, who otherwise never contradicted her, shook her head and whimpered and kept pointing at the hearth, Lene said: 'Mother, you know me better than that! I won't take your hearth and your fire away from you; you'll have everything the same again; I've got enough money saved up, and even if I hadn't I'd work till I had. But we must get away from here. I have to go past there every day, and it's more than I can take, mother. I don't begrudge him his happiness; in fact I'm glad for him, I swear to God, because he was a good, dear man and did what he could to make me happy, and never any arrogance or grand airs. And to put it plainly, even though I can't bear fine gentlemen normally, he was a true nobleman, one who really had his heart in the right place. Yes, my own beloved Botho, you be happy, as happy as you deserve. But I can't be a witness to it, mother. I have to get away from here, otherwise every time I walk ten paces I'll be afraid of seeing him in front of me. I'll be a bundle of nerves. No, no, I can't have that. But you'll still have your seat by the hearth. It's me, your Lene, who's promising you that.'

After this conversation the old woman had given up all resistance, and Frau Dörr too had said, 'Course you'll have to move out. An' as for Dörr, serve him right, it will, the old skinflint! He was always grumblin' to me that you were lodged there too cheap, an' that the rent didn't cover the rates and the upkeep. Now we'll see how it suits him to have the place empty. An' that's what'll happen, 'cos who's goin' to move into a shoe-box like that, where every cat can look in at the window, and no gas or mains water? You've got three months' notice, of course, so you can leave at Easter, whatever fuss he makes. An' I'm truly glad of it – yes, Lene, that's how wicked I am! Mind you I'll have to pay for my bit of spite, 'cos when you've gone, my girl, and dear Frau Nimptsch with her fire an' her kettle always on the boil – well, Lene, what'll I have left? Just *him* and Sultan and the stupid boy, who gets more stupid each day. And no other livin' soul. And when it turns cold and the snow comes, then the loneliness of sittin' around with nothin' to do is more than a Christian body can bear.'

These were the first discussions that had followed Lene's resolve to move away, and her plan was carried through one day around Easter when a removal wagon arrived to load up such goods as they possessed. Old Dörr had behaved surprisingly well to the last, and after they had all solemnly said goodbye Frau Nimptsch was packed into a cab with her squirrel and her goldfinch and driven across to the Luisenufer,* where

---

* An area of new buildings along the west bank of the Luisenstädtischer Kanal, dug in 1849.

Lene had taken an excellent little apartment three floors up. Not only had she purchased some new furniture, but, above all, she had honoured her promise by having a hearth built onto the large stove in the front room. At first the landlord had made all sorts of difficulties about this, saying that such an addition would ruin the stove. However, Lene had insisted, at the same time giving her reasons, and this had made such a positive impression on the landlord, a worthy old master joiner, that he was moved to yield to her wishes.

The two women now lived much as they had in the Dörrs' garden-house, except that they were now three floors up and looked out, not on the fantastical turrets of the Elephant House, but on the pretty dome of St Michael's Church. It was indeed a delightful view to have, and so beautiful and unimpeded that it even began to exert an influence on the habits of old Frau Nimptsch, inducing her, when the sun shone, to exchange her place on the footstool by the fire for one by the open window, where Lene had installed a low seat for her. All this made the old woman feel infinitely better and also benefited her health, so that following the move she was less subject to rheumatism than she had been in the garden-house, which, for all its romantic situation, had been little more than a cellar.

Besides, never a week went by without a visit from Frau Dörr, who walked from the Zoological Gardens to the Luisenufer despite the enormous distance between them 'just to see how things were'. In the manner typical of all Berlin housewives she would then speak of nothing but her husband, regularly falling into a tone that implied that her marriage to him was a terrible misalliance and really almost unaccountable. The truth of the matter was that she was not only exceedingly comfortable and contented, but positively glad that Dörr was exactly as he was. She could only gain from this, most obviously in constantly getting richer, but also, and to her just as importantly, in being able ceaselessly to set herself above the old miser and reprove him for his base-mindedness without any risk of changing his ways or of the pecuniary loss this would have entailed. Dörr, then, was the main topic of these conversations, and unless she was at Goldsteins' or elsewhere in town Lene always heartily joined in the laughter, all the more for the fact that, like Frau Nimptsch, she had visibly recruited strength since the move. The business of procuring what they needed for the apartment and making it ready to move into had from the outset naturally distracted her from her brooding, and even more important, particularly for her health and emotional recovery, was that she no longer needed to fear an encounter with Botho. Who ever came to the Luisenufer? Certainly not Botho. All this combined to make Lene look fresher and more cheerful again, and only one outward sign remained of the struggles she had gone through: a strand of white hair drawn from her parting. Frau Nimptsch did not notice or made little of it, but Frau Dörr, who in her own way was a follower of fashion and above all extremely proud of her braids of real hair, spotted the white strand immediately and remarked to Lene, 'Lord, Lene! An' on the left too. But of course ... that's the side ... so it had to be on the left.'

This conversation took place soon after the move. Otherwise Botho and the time with him were generally not brought up, for the simple reason that whenever the talk turned to this particular topic Lene quickly broke it off or even left the room. After this had occurred a number of times Frau Dörr noticed it and from then on held her tongue on matters that the other woman quite clearly wanted neither to talk nor hear about. This went on for a year, and after that there was another reason why it would have seemed inadvisable to hark back to that episode. The next-door apartment, wall to wall with Frau Nimptsch's, had been occupied by a new tenant, who from the start cultivated good neighbourly relations and soon promised to become more than just a good neighbour. Every evening he came over to chat, and some-times it was quite like the days when Dörr had sat on his stool smoking his pipe, except that the new neighbour was different in many respects: a cultivated man of orderly habits with respectful manners, though not exactly refined, and an able conversationalist, who if Lene was present would speak of various municipal affairs, of schools, gasworks and drainage systems, and sometimes also of his travels. He was not put out if he happened to find the old woman alone, and played rummy or draughts with her or helped her lay out a game of patience, even though he abhorred all card games. He was in fact a Dissenter, and after having been active among the Mennonites and later the Irvingites he had recently founded an independent sect.

As may be imagined, all this aroused the liveliest curi-osity in Frau Dörr, who never tired of asking questions and dropping hints, but only if Lene was busy about the apart-ment or running her various errands in town. 'Tell me, Frau Nimptsch, my dear, what is he exactly? I looked him up but he wasn't in yet; Dörr's only ever got last year's. His name's Franke, isn't it?'

'Yes, Franke.'

'Franke. There used to be someone called that in the Ohmgasse, a master cooper, an' he only had one eye. I mean, the other one was still there, but all white, and looked jus' like an air bladder on a fish. And d'you know why? A hoop he was tryin' to fit snapped back and the point went straight in his eye. That's why. I wonder if it's the same family.'

'No, Frau Dörr, he's not from here at all. He's from Bremen.'

'Oh, I see. Well, that makes sense then.'

Frau Nimptsch nodded, without seeking further clarifica-tion as to what it was that made sense. 'An' from Bremen to America only takes a fortnight, so that's where he went. An' he was a plumber or a locksmith or a machinist, something like that, but when he saw he wasn't gettin' anywhere he became a doctor and went about with lots of little bottles, an' apparently he did some preachin' too. And because he preached so well he got a job with . . . Oh, I forget the name of it now. But apparently they were all very God-fearing people and very respectable.'

'Goodness gracious me!' said Frau Dörr. 'Don't tell me he's . . . Lord, what are they called, the ones with lots of wives, always six or seven apiece, an' even more some of 'em. What they do with so many I don't know.'

It was a subject after Frau Dörr's heart, but her friend reassured her by saying, 'No, Frau Dörr, my dear, that's somethin' else. At first I thought it might be that, but he laughed and said, "Heaven forbid, Frau Nimptsch! I'm a bachelor. And if I do get married I think one'll do just fine."'

'Well, that takes a load off my mind,' said Frau Dörr. 'An' what happened after that? Over in America, I mean.'

'Well, after that things went very well, and it wasn't long before he got the help he needed. That's what those godly folk are, always helpin' each other out. An' he got customers again and went back to his old trade. And that's what he still does, an' he's in a big factory in the Köpenickerstrasse, where they make little pipes and burners and stopcocks an' everthin' else they need for gas. An' he's the top man, somethin' like a carpenters' or masons' foreman, with about a hundred under him. An' he's a very respectable man, with a top hat and black gloves. Got a good salary too.'

'And what about Lene?'

'Oh, she'd have him all right. An' why not? But she can't keep mum, an' if he comes to say his piece then she'll tell him everything about the past, first with Kuhlwein (which is so long ago it might as well never have been) and then the baron. An' you have to understand, Franke's a very fine an' upright man, pretty well a gen'l'man by now.'

'We'll have to talk her out of it. He doesn't need to know

everythin'; why should he? We don't know everythin', do we?'
'True enough; but our Lene ...'

18

IT WAS NOW June 1878. Frau von Rienäcker and Frau von
Sellenthin had spent May on a visit to the young couple, and
with each passing day both mother and mother-in-law had
become more firmly persuaded that their Käthe appeared
paler, more anaemic, and more languid than usual, and not
surprisingly they unceasingly urged her to see a specialist.
With his help, and incidentally after very costly gynaecological examinations, it was deemed imperative as a first measure
that she take a four-week cure at Schlangenbad. After that she
could go to Schwalbach. Käthe had laughed and rejected the
whole idea, most of all the resort, saying that Schlangenbad
was such an uncanny name and she could almost feel a
viper at her breast. Eventually she had yielded, and found
a satisfaction in the initial preparations for the journey that
exceeded any she anticipated from the cure itself. Every day
she drove into town to make purchases, and never wearied
of declaring that now for the first time she understood why
'shopping', as she said in English, stood in such high favour
and esteem with English ladies; wandering from shop to shop
and finding nothing but pretty things and polite people was
a real pleasure, she said, and instructive too, because you
saw so much that you had never seen or indeed even heard
of before. As a rule Botho accompanied her on these drives
and walks, and well before the last week in June half the
Rienäckers' apartment had been transformed into a small
exhibition of travelling paraphernalia. The prime exhibit
was an enormous trunk with brass mountings, which Botho
not entirely unjustly described as the 'coffin of his fortune';

then came two smaller trunks of Russia leather, together with bags, blankets and cushions, while spread out over the sofa was the travel costume, with a dustcoat taking pride of place alongside a pair of wonderfully thick-soled lace-up boots, as if what was being planned was a glacier-climbing expedition.

With her departure fixed for 24th June, Midsummer Day, Käthe decided to gather the *cercle intime* around her one last time on the evening before, and so Wedell, one of the young Ostens, and of course Pitt and Serge were invited for a relatively early hour. Also present was her particular favourite Balafré, who had ridden in the great cavalry charge at Mars-la-Tour as a member of his old regiment, the Halberstadt Cuirassiers, and received a mighty blow that left the gash across his brow and cheek to which he owed his nickname.

Käthe sat between Wedell and Balafré, and did not look as if she was in great need of Schlangenbad or indeed any other waters in the world. She had a good colour, laughed, asked scores of questions, and was quite content with just the first few words of any answer she received. It was she who dominated the conversation, which no one minded as she was a truly consummate practitioner of the art of aimless but winsome chatter. Balafré asked how she imagined her daily life during her curative sojourn. Schlangenbad, he remarked, was famous not just for its therapeutic wonders, but much, much more so for its tedium, and four weeks of spa-town tedium was rather a lot to endure, however beneficial the waters might be.

'My dear Balafré,' replied Käthe, 'you mustn't frighten me like that, nor would you if you knew how much Botho has done for me. He's packed eight volumes of novellas in my trunk, admittedly right at the bottom, and just in case my imagination gets overheated and harms the effects of the cure he's also slipped in a book on advanced fish-farming.'

Balafré laughed.

'You may laugh, my dear friend, but you don't know

the half of it. The main thing is his motivation (because Botho never does anything without good reason). Of course I was only joking just now when I said the brochure on fish-farming was to stop my imagination overheating, his real, serious object is that I *must* at long last get round to reading this kind of thing–the brochure, I mean–out of regional pride, because the Neumark, our common happy home, has apparently long been the breeding-ground and birthplace of advanced fish-farming, and if I continue to be ignorant of this new means of nutrition so essential to the local economy, I can't possibly show my face east of the Oder in the Landsberg District, and least of all in Berneuchen at my cousin Borne's.'

Botho made to speak, but she cut him short. 'I know what you're going to say, and that as for the eight novellas they're only there as a last resort. Of course, of course, you're always so terribly cautious. But I can't see that there'll be any need for "last resorts". You see, only yesterday I had a letter from my sister Ine, who tells me that Anna Grävenitz has been there for a week now. You know her, Wedell, one of the Rohr girls, a charming blonde; I was with her at Fräulein Zülow's school, in the same class in fact. I can still remember how we both worshipped our idol Felix Bachmann[*] and even wrote verses to him, until the good old Fräulein said she wouldn't stand for such nonsense. And according to Ine Elly Winterfeld will probably come too. Now I can't help thinking that in the company of two delightful young ladies–with myself as a third, though not at all comparable with the other two–in such good company, I say, surely the time must pass tolerably. Don't you agree, my dear Balafré?'

The latter bowed with an exaggerated facial expression that was meant to convey his assent to everything except the notion that there was anyone alive with whom she could not

---

[*] I.e. the popular *Heldentenor* Eduard Bachmann, who eventually lost his voice and committed suicide in 1880.

be advantageously compared. He nonetheless persisted with his original inquiry: 'If I might hear details, gracious lady. It's the particular things that fill each minute, so to speak, that determine whether we are happy or not. And a day contains so many minutes!'

'Well, I imagine it like this. Every morning correspondence, and then a promenade concert and a walk with the two ladies, preferably in a secluded avenue. Then we'll sit down and read one another the letters I trust we'll receive, and if our husbands write affectionately we'll laugh and say "Ah, yes". Then comes taking the waters, and after that we'll dress for the evening, naturally with great love and care, which can't be any less fun in Schlangenbad than it is in Berlin. On the contrary. And then we'll go in to dine, and have an old general on our right and a wealthy industrialist on our left. I've had a passion for industrialists ever since I was a young girl, and I'm not a bit ashamed of it. I mean, either they've invented a new type of armour plating or laid telegraph cables on the sea bed or bored a tunnel or built a funicular railway. Besides which they're rich, which I don't despise either. And after dinner a coffee in the reading room with the blinds lowered, so that the light and shadows keep dancing across the page of the newspaper. And then a drive. And perhaps, if we're lucky, a few officers from Frankfurt or Mainz might stray over in our direction and ride alongside our carriage; and I must tell you, gentlemen, that you can't compete with hussars, the red or the blue, and from my own military standpoint I shall always consider it a decided error to have doubled the strength of the dragoons but left the hussars as they were. And it amazes me even more that they're left so far away. Something as stylish as that belongs in the capital.'

Botho was beginning to feel embarrassed by his wife's tremendous facility of speech, and sought to contain her chatter with little teasing remarks. But his guests were far less critical than he, indeed they were more amused than

ever by the 'delightful little woman', and Balafré, who led
the field in Käthe worship, said, 'Rienäcker, another word
against your wife and you're a dead man. My gracious lady,
what does this ogre of a husband want? What's he carping
about? I can't imagine. The only thing I can think of is that
you've wounded his pride as a heavy cavalryman, and, if
you'll excuse the pun, he's up in arms to defend his heavy
armour. Rienäcker, I implore you! If I had a wife like yours
I'd obey her every whim, and if the gracious lady would have
me a hussar I should become one without further ado. But
there's one thing I do know, and I'd gladly stake my life and
honour on it, which is that if His Majesty could hear such an
eloquent appeal, the hussar guards wouldn't have a moment's
peace in their barracks; by tomorrow they'd be bivouacked in
Zehlendorf, and the next day they'd be marching through the
Brandenburg Gate into the city! Oh, these Sellenthins – and
now I'll take opportunity by the forelock and raise my glass
to them once, twice, and thrice! Why haven't you any more
sisters for us, my gracious lady? Why is Fräulein Ine already
engaged? Far too soon and a most grievous blow to me.'

Käthe, always happy with little tributes of this sort, assured
him that while Ine was of course irretrievably lost to him she
would do whatever she could to help, although she knew
perfectly well that he was an incorrigible bachelor and didn't
mean a word of it. Presently she dropped this bantering
exchange with Balafré and resumed speaking of her journey,
especially of how she envisaged her correspondence while
she was away. She reiterated her hope that she would receive
a letter every day, which it was certainly the duty of an affectionate husband to provide, but for her part would be guided
by events, committing herself only to give a sign of life at
each stopping point on the first day. This suggestion met with
approval, even from Rienäcker, and was only later modified
so that while she would still write a card at all the main stopping points as far as Cologne, which was on her route despite

representing a detour, she now planned to put all her cards, however many or few there might be, into a single envelope. This had the advantage, she said, of permitting her to express herself with complete freedom on the subject of her travelling companions without having to worry about the prying eyes of mail-dispatching clerks and postmen.

After dinner they drank coffee out on the balcony, giving Käthe, who had resisted their entreaties for a while, a chance to present herself to the others in her travel costume, with a Rembrandt hat and dustcoat together with a travelling bag slung over her shoulder. She looked delightful. Balafré was more captivated than ever, and begged her not to be too surprised if she found him next morning pressed into a corner of the compartment and timidly offering to escort her on the journey.

'Provided he can get leave,' laughed Pitt.

'Or deserts,' added Serge, 'just to make the act of homage complete.'

They chatted on in this vein for a while, and then the guests said goodbye to their amiable hosts and agreed to accompany one another as far as the Lützowplatz Bridge. Then the party divided into two, with Balafré, Wedell and Osten continuing their leisurely course along the canal while Pitt and Serge, who intended to go on to the Kroll Gardens, headed for the Tiergarten.

'Charming creature, Käthe,' said Serge. 'Rienäcker looks a pretty dull dog next to her, and sometimes he puts on such a peevish, know-all face as if he had to make excuses for the little woman to everyone in the room, whereas in actual fact she's cleverer than he is.'

Pitt said nothing.

'And what's she going to Schwalbach or Schlangenbad for?' continued Serge. 'It doesn't help, and if it does then it's mostly help of a pretty rum kind.'

Pitt gave him a sideways glance. 'Serge, I find you're

getting more russified by the day; or, to put it another way, you're growing more and more into your name.'

'Nothing like enough. But joking aside, my friend, one thing is serious: I'm vexed with Rienäcker. What's he got against his delightful little wife? Any idea?'

'Yes.'

'What then?'

'She's a little bit silly,' replied Pitt in English. 'Or, if you'd rather hear it in German, she prattles on rather. Too much for *him* at any rate.'

19

BEFORE HER TRAIN had even got from Berlin to Potsdam Käthe pulled the yellow curtains across her compartment window to protect herself against the intensifying glare; however, the curtains were open that same day in the apartment on the Luisenufer, and the late morning sun shone brightly through Frau Nimptsch's windows, filling the whole room with light. Only the farthest area lay in shadow, and here stood an old-fashioned bed with red-and-white-checked pillows piled up high to support Frau Nimptsch. She was rather sitting than lying, for she had water on the lungs and suffered gravely from asthma. She kept turning her head to the one open window, but even more often to the stove, which had no fire burning in its hearth today.

Lene sat beside her, holding her hand, and when she saw the old woman look constantly in the same direction, she said, 'Shall I light a fire, mother? I thought that since you're lying down with the bed warming you and since it's so hot ...'

The old woman said nothing, but it appeared to Lene that she had guessed her wishes correctly. So she crossed the room, bent down, and lit a fire.

When she returned to the bed, the old woman was smiling contentedly. 'Yes Lene, it is hot. But you know I always like to see it. An' when I can't I start thinkin' it's all over – no more life, not even a spark. An' I do get frightened, 'cos of this ...'

And she pointed to her chest and heart.

'Oh, mother, you always think you're about to die. And yet it's passed off again often enough.'

'Yes, my child, it's often passed off again, but the time'll come, an' at seventy it could come any day. Just open the other window as well. That'll let more air in and the fire'll take better. Looks like it's givin' up; it's smokin' so much ...'

'That's because the sun's shining straight onto it.'

'An' then give me some of the green drops that Frau Dörr brought. They always help a bit.'

Lene did as she was bidden, and when the sick woman had taken the drops she did indeed seem somewhat better and easier in her mind. She braced her hand against the bed and raised herself up, and after Lene had stuffed another cushion under the small of her back she said, 'Has Franke been yet?'

'Yes, first thing this morning. He always asks after you before he's off to the factory.'

'He's a very good man.'

'Yes, he is.'

'An' as for that sect business ...'

'That's not such a problem. And I almost think that's where he gets his good principles from. Don't you agree?'

The old woman smiled. 'No, Lene, they come from the Good Lord. Some folks have 'em and some don't. I don't believe you can get 'em from teachers or books ... An' hasn't he said anythin' yet?'

'Yes, last night.'

'And what did you answer him?'

'I said I'd accept him, because I thought he was an honest, dependable man who'd take care of me, but also of you ...'

The old woman nodded in agreement.

'And once I'd said that,' Lene continued, 'he took my hand and exclaimed full of joy, "Well Lene, that's settled then!" But I shook my head and said it wasn't that simple, because there was something I had to confess to him. And when he asked what it was I told him that I'd had two previous relationships: first ... well, you know, mother ... the first man I was really fond of, and the second one I'd loved deeply, and my heart still pined for him. But he was now happily married, and I'd never seen him again, except just once, and nor did I want to see him again. I said that I had to tell him all this because he'd been so kind to us, and because I didn't want to deceive anyone, least of all him ...'

'Lord, Lord,' whimpered the old woman as Lene spoke.

'... and straight after I'd said that he got up and went back to his apartment. But he wasn't angry, I could clearly see that. Only he wouldn't let me walk him to his hall door like I normally do.'

Frau Nimptsch was visibly frightened and agitated, though it was hard to tell whether this was caused by what she had just heard or by her breathing difficulties. The latter almost seemed more likely, because all at once she said, 'Lene my child, I'm not raised up enough. You'll have to slip the hymn book under me.'

Lene did not demur, but went to fetch the hymn book. However, when she brought it the old woman said, 'No, not that one, that's the new one. It's the old one I want, the thick one with two clasps.' And once Lene had returned with the thick hymn book she went on, 'I had to fetch it for my mother too, God rest her soul. I was still half a child at the time, an' my mother not even fifty, an' it'd got her the same way an' she couldn't breathe, jus' kept starin' at me with big frightened eyes. But as soon as I slipped the Porst hymn book under her that she got when she was confirmed she became calm and then passed away peacefully. An' that's what I want to do. Oh, Lene. It's not death ... It's the dyin' ... There, there. Ah, that's better.'

Lene wept softly, and as it was plain that the kind old woman's last hour was near she sent a message to Frau Dörr that things were serious and could she please come. Frau Dörr sent the reply that she would, and at the sixth hour she duly appeared with much noise and commotion, because being quiet, even at a sick bed, was not her way. She stomped across the room so that everything on and near the hearth trembled and rattled, and complained about her husband, who was always in town when he was needed at home, and always at home when she wished he would go to the devil. As she spoke she pressed the sick woman's hand and asked Lene if she had given her plenty of drops.

'Yes.'

'How many?'

'Five ... five every two hours.'

That was too little, Frau Dörr assured her, before reaching into all the recesses of her medical expertise and adding that she had left the drops to draw in the sun for a fortnight, and if they were taken correctly the fluid would be drawn off as if by a pump. Old Selke over by the Zoological Gardens had been like a barrel, and for a whole three months he'd never had sight of his bed sheets, always sitting up straight in his chair with the windows all wide open, but once he'd taken the drops for four days it was like squeezing a pig's bladder: hadn't she seen it, everything flushing out in a jiffy and then just a bag of loose skin.

With these words the sturdy woman forced old Frau Nimptsch to take a double dose of her foxglove mixture.

At the sight of this energetic assistance Lene quite justifiably felt even more anxious than before, so she took up her shawl and got ready to go and fetch a doctor. And Frau Dörr, who was usually against all doctors, made no objection this time.

'Go on,' she said, 'she hasn't got long now. Jus' look

there' – and she pointed to the sides of the sick woman's nose – 'that's the mark of death.'

Lene set out, but she could barely have reached St Michael's Church Square when the old woman, who until then had been dozing as she lay, pulled herself up and called for her: 'Lene …'

'Lene's not here.'

'Who's that then?'

'It's me, Mother Nimptsch. Frau Dörr.'

'Ah, Frau Dörr, that's good. Move up closer, here on the footstool.'

Frau Dörr was quite unaccustomed to taking orders and jibbed a little, but she was too good-natured not to obey, and so she sat down on the stool.

And behold, even as she did so the old woman began to speak: 'I want a yellow coffin with blue mounting. But not too much …'

'Right, Frau Nimptsch.'

'An' I want to be buried in the New St James' Cemetery, beyond the Rollkrug an' well over towards Britz.'

'Right, Frau Nimptsch.'

'An' I've saved everythin' for it, many years ago when I still could. It's in the top drawer. An' you'll also find the shift there an' the camisole, an' a pair of white stockin's with an 'N' on them. An' that's where it is.'

'Right, Frau Nimptsch. It'll all be jus' as you've said. Is there anythin' else?'

But the old woman appeared not to hear Frau Dörr any more, and without answering she joined her hands together, looked up to the ceiling with a devout, kindly expression, and prayed: 'Dear Father in Heaven, take her into Your safe-keeping and reward her for all the things she's done for a poor old woman.'

'Ah yes, Lene,' said Frau Dörr to herself, and then added aloud: 'That's jus' what the Good Lord'll do, Frau Nimptsch.

I know His ways, an' I've never seen no one come to grief who had such a good heart an' a care for others as our Lene.'

The old woman nodded, and in her mind a benevolent image came clearly into view.

The minutes went by, and when Lene returned and knocked on the front door from the corridor, Frau Dörr was still sitting on the footstool holding her old friend's hand. And only now that she heard the knocking outside did she release it, and stood up to open the door.

Lene was still out of breath. 'He's just coming … he'll be here any minute.'

'Doctors indeed,' was all Frau Dörr said, and she pointed to the dead woman.

20

KÄTHE'S first letter was posted from Cologne and arrived in Berlin as promised on the following morning. It came in the addressed envelope Botho had provided, and felt quite thick as he held it, smiling and good-humoured, in his hands. The envelope contained no less than three cards written on both sides in faint pencil, all of them so hard to read that he stepped out onto the balcony the better to decipher the elusive scrawl.

'Now let's see, Käthe.'

And he read:

Brandenburg on the Havel, 8 am
The train only stops here for three minutes, my dear Botho, but they shall not be wasted, and if need be I'll carry on writing as best I can when we're moving again. I'm travelling with a young, very charming banker's wife, Madame Salinger, née Saling, from Vienna. When I expressed

surprise at the similarity of the two names, she said in a
thick Viennese accent, 'Well, don't you see, I married my
comparative.' She comes out with things like this the whole
time, and despite having a ten-year-old daughter (blonde,
the mother brunette) she too is going to Schlangenbad.
She is also going via Cologne, like me, to pay a visit there.
The child is sweet-tempered but not well brought up, and
by constantly clambering around the compartment she has
already broken my parasol, which greatly embarrassed her
mother. The station we're at now (in fact just this instant
the train is pulling out again) is teeming with soldiers,
among them Brandenburg Cuirassiers with quince-yellow
monograms on their epaulettes, probably Tsar Nicholas
regiment. It looks very smart. There were fusiliers too,
Thirty-Fifth, small men who seemed rather smaller than
they ought to be, though Uncle Kurt Anton always used
to say that the best fusilier is the one you can only spot
through field glasses. But I'll close now. The little girl is
still racing from one compartment window to the other,
I'm afraid, which makes it difficult to write. At the same
time she is forever munching bits of cake, little slices
of cherry tart with pistachio nuts. She started on these
between Potsdam and Werder. Her mother really is too
soft. I'd be stricter.'

Botho laid the card aside and ran through as much as he could
read of the second. It went as follows:

Hanover, 12.30
Goltz was on the platform at Magdeburg and said you had
written that I was coming. How sweet and kind of you yet
again! You are always the best and most thoughtful of men.
Goltz has now got the surveying of the Harz Mountains,
that is to say he starts on 1st July. Here in Hanover we
have a fifteen-minute stop, which I have used to look at

the square right next to the station: nothing but hotels and beer halls built since our rule began here, one of them in an entirely Gothic style. A fellow passenger told me that the Hanoverians call it the 'Prussian Beer Church' out of sheer Guelphic antagonism.[*] How painful such things are! But even *here* time will be a great healer. God grant that it is. – The little girl is still nibbling away, which is starting to make me feel uneasy. Where will it end? Her mother is truly charming, however, and has told me *everything*. She has already been to Würzburg to see the obstetrician Scanzoni and raves about him. The way she confides in me is embarrassing, rather awkward even. Aside from that she is, I can only repeat, thoroughly *comme il faut*. Just to mention one point, you should see her dressing case! The Viennese really are far ahead of us in that kind of thing; that's where the older culture comes through.

'Wonderful,' Botho laughed. 'When Käthe starts making observations about history and culture she surpasses herself. But all good things come in threes. Let's see.'

And he took up the third card.

Cologne, 8 pm. Military Governor's Residence
On reflection I think I'll post my cards *here* rather than wait till I get to Schlangenbad, where Frau Salinger and I expect to arrive midday tomorrow. I'm well. Herr and Frau von Schroffenstein very amiable, he particularly. Incidentally, I must not omit to mention that Frau Salinger was met at the station by an Oppenheim[†] carriage. From Hamm onwards our journey, which had started so delight-

---

[*] In 1866 Prussia annexed the kingdom of Hanover, an ally of defeated Austria in the war of that year. The strong anti-Prussian feeling this aroused was expressed in an attachment to the deposed royal house of Welf (or Guelph).
[†] A Jewish banking firm prominent in the nineteenth century.

fully, became somewhat tiresome and disagreeable. The little girl was unwell, unfortunately her mother's fault. 'What else would you like?' she asked after the train had just passed Hamm station, to which the child replied, 'fruit drops.' And *that* was the moment it all started to go wrong ... Ah, my dear Botho, young or old, we need to subject our desires to a strict and scrupulous discipline. This thought has been preoccupying me unceasingly since what happened, and perhaps meeting this charming woman was no accident in my life. How often have I heard Kluckhuhn speak along these lines. And he's quite right. More tomorrow. – Your Käthe.

Botho slipped the three cards back in the envelope and said to himself, 'Käthe through and through. What a flair she has for gossip! Maybe I should be pleased that she writes as she does. But there's something missing. It's all so glib, just an echo of society talk. But she'll change once she has responsibilities. Or she might. I can at least hope she will.'

The following day brought a short letter from Schlangenbad with far, far less matter than the three cards, and thereafter Käthe only wrote twice a week, mainly to gossip about Anna Grävenitz and Elly Winterfeld, who had indeed materialized, and most of all about Madame Salinger and sweet little Sarah. The views she expressed about them remained the same, and only at the end of the third week was there something of a change of tone:

I now find the little girl more charming than her mother, who indulges in a luxury of dress that I hardly think proper, especially as there are no gentlemen here to speak of. I also now see that she wears make-up, in particular colouring her eyebrows and perhaps her lips too, for they are cherry-red. The child, however, is very natural. Whenever she sees me she dashes up impetuously and kisses my hand

and apologizes for the hundredth time about the fruit drops, saying that her Mama was to blame – I have to agree with her there! But there must be some mysterious gluttonous streak in Sarah's nature, I might almost say something like original sin (do you believe in that? I do, my dear Botho), for she cannot stop eating sweet things and is always buying herself wafer cakes – not the Berlin type, which taste like cream puffs, but the Carlsbad ones with sprinklings of sugar. But no more of this in writing. We shall speak of this and much else besides when I see you, which may be very soon as I should like to travel with Anna Grävenitz – it's to be with one's own kind. Oh, how I look forward to seeing you again and being able to sit out on the balcony with you! Berlin really is the best place of all, and how glorious it is when the sun sinks behind the Charlottenburg Palace and the Grunewald and a sleepy, dreamy mood takes hold of you! Don't you agree? And can you guess what Frau Salinger said to me yesterday? She said I had grown even fairer than before. Well, you shall soon see for youself. – Ever yours, Käthe.

Rienäcker nodded his head and smiled: 'Charming little woman. Not a word about her treatment; I'll wager she's been going out for drives and hasn't even taken the waters ten times.' After saying this to himself he gave instructions to his batman, who had just entered the room, and then went out, crossing the Tiergarten to the Brandenburg Gate and then going down Unter den Linden towards his barracks, where he was on duty until midday.

He got back home just past twelve, and after a bite to eat was settling down to relax when his batman came to say that there was a 'gentleman' ... a 'man' (he wavered between the two words) outside who wanted to speak to the Herr Baron.

'Who is he?'

'Gideon Franke ... That's what he said.'

'Franke? That's odd. Never heard of him. Have him come in.'

The batman went out again, while Botho repeated to himself, 'Franke ... Gideon Franke ... Never heard of him. Don't know him.'

An instant later the visitor entered and bowed rather stiffly just inside the door. He wore a black-brown coat buttoned up to the top and inordinately shiny boots, and his shiny black hair was combed flat over his temples. Black gloves and a high stand-up collar of irreproachable whiteness completed the picture.

Botho went forward to meet him with his characteristic chivalrous courtesy. 'Herr Franke?' he asked.

The other man nodded.

'How can I be of service? Would you care to take a seat? ... Here ... Or maybe here. Upholstered chairs are never as comfortable as they look.'

Franke assented with a smile and sat down on the cane chair Rienäcker had indicated to him.

'How can I be of service?' Rienäcker repeated.

'I've come to ask a question, Herr Baron.'

'Which it will be my pleasure to answer, provided I can answer it.'

'Oh, none better than you, Herr von Rienäcker ... You see, I've come about Lene Nimptsch.'

Botho started back.

'... And I should like, if I may, to add straight away that there's nothing indelicate in the business that brings me here. Nothing that I wish to say, or, if you'll permit me, Herr Baron, to ask, will cause any embarrassment to you or your family. I am also aware that your gracious lady, the baroness, is away from home, and I have been most particular about waiting until I could find you alone—as a grass widower, if I may put it thus.'

With his fine ear for such things Botho discerned that his interlocutor was, for all his starchily bourgeois attire, an independent-minded man of honourable character. This aided him in rapidly overcoming his perplexity, and it was with his calmness and composure more or less restored that he leant across the table and asked, 'Are you a relative of Lene's? Forgive me, Herr Franke, if I call my old friend by the name, so dear to me, that I've always used.'

Franke bowed and replied, 'No, Herr Baron, I'm not a relative. I can't claim that prerogative. But my prerogative is perhaps quite as good: I have known Lene for a long while now and have formed the intention of marrying her. Moreover she has given her consent, but in doing so she told me of her past, speaking with such great affection of yourself that I at once resolved to come and ask you quite openly and candidly, Herr Baron, how I am to regard Lene. And when I informed Lene herself she encouraged me in my intention with obvious pleasure, only adding that perhaps I should refrain as you would speak too well of her.'

Botho stared straight ahead and struggled to master his emotions. At last his self-possession returned, and he said, 'You're a decent man, Herr Franke, who only wants what's best for Lene – that much I can see and hear – and so you have every right to an answer. There's no doubt in my mind as to what I have to say to you, and the only thing that gives me pause is *how* I should say it. The best thing is if I tell you how it all started, how it went on, and then how it ended.'

Franke bowed once more to signal that he too considered this the best course.

'Well,' Rienäcker began, 'it's three years ago now or maybe a few months more. I was on a rowing outing near Lovers' Island at Treptow and found myself in a position to be of service to two young girls by preventing their boat from capsizing. One of the girls was Lene, and from the way she thanked me I could immediately tell there was something different about her. There were no empty phrases at all–neither then nor later, which I'd like to emphasize straight away, because although she can be cheerful and at times exuberant, by nature she's thoughtful, serious and straightforward.'

Mechanically Botho pushed the tray that was still on the table to one side, smoothed the tablecloth with his hand, and then continued, 'I asked leave to escort her home and she granted it without further ado, which for a moment rather surprised me. You see, I didn't know her yet. Very soon, though, I saw what lay behind it: from early youth she'd been in the habit of acting by her own lights, without paying too much attention to others and certainly without worrying what they might think.'

Franke nodded.

'So I accompanied her on the long walk back to her home and was captivated by everything I saw there: the old lady, the hearth she was sitting at, the garden around the house, and the seclusion and tranquillity of the whole place. After a quarter of an hour I left, and as I said goodbye to Lene outside at the garden gate I asked if I might come again, to which she replied with a simple 'yes'. No false modesty, but also nothing remotely unfeminine. On the contrary, there was something touching in her voice and manner.'

Rienäcker, visibly moved as these images all took shape again in his mind, stood up and opened both of the balcony doors as if the room had become too warm for him. Then, pacing back and forth, he continued speaking at a faster pace: 'I've got little else to add. That was around Easter, and for the whole summer we had the happiest of days. Should I tell you about them? No. And then the serious realities of life made their claim on us, and that's what forced us to separate.'

Botho had by now sat down again, and Franke, who had been occupied the whole time in smoothing his hat, said quietly, 'Yes, that's what she told me too.'

'Yes, and it can't be otherwise, Herr Franke. You see, Lene—and it does my heart good to be able to say this as well—Lene doesn't lie, and she'd rather bite her own tongue off than tell a fib. She's got a twofold pride, firstly that of living by her own labour, and along with that the pride of always talking straight without any evasions or making things out to be more or less than they really are. "I don't need to, and I don't *want* to"—I've heard her say that many times. Yes, she's got a will of her own, maybe a little more than she should have, and anyone wanting to find fault with her could accuse her of being headstrong. But she only ever wants what she believes she can answer for and most likely can answer for, and to my mind that sort of will is more force of character than self-righteousness. You're nodding, and that shows me we're of the same opinion, at which I sincerely rejoice. And now just one final thought, Herr Franke. What's past is past. If you can't see your way to overlooking it, I'd have to respect that. But if you can, I tell you you'll have an uncommonly good wife in her. Because her heart's in the right place and she's got a strong sense of duty and justice and order.'

'That's how I've always found Lene too, and I expect, just as you say, Herr Baron, that I shall have an uncommonly good wife in her. Yes, people should keep the Commandments, they should keep them *all*, but there's a difference according to the Commandment in question. He who fails to keep *one* of them may still be worthy, but there's *another* that stands right next to it in the catechism, and he who fails to keep that one is worth nothing; he is damned from the outset and stands outside God's grace.'*

Botho looked at him in amazement, clearly not knowing what to make of this solemn oration. But Gideon Franke, having now warmed to his theme, had no care for the impres-

---

* The Commandments to which Franke refers are, respectively, 'Thou shalt not commit adultery' and 'Thou shalt not bear false witness'.

sion his thoroughly homebred dogmas produced, and therefore continued in an increasingly sermonizing tone: 'And
he who in the weakness of his flesh breaks the sixth may be
forgiven provided that he repents and reforms his life; but
he who breaks the *seventh* shows not just the weakness of his
flesh but the baseness of his soul, and he who lies and cheats
and slanders and bears false witness is corrupt to his core,
born of darkness and with no hope of salvation, he is like a
field so polluted with nettles that however much good corn is
sown in it they will always spring up anew. And by this conviction, and by the experience of all my days, I shall live and die.
Yes, Herr Baron, it's a question of decency, it's a question of
sincerity, and it's a question of integrity. In married life too.
For honesty is the best policy, and our pledged word must be
our bond. What has been has been, and is for God to judge.
And if I thought differently of the matter, which I would
also respect, just as you would yourself, Herr Baron, then I
would have to leave off and not even begin to speak words of
love and affection. I spent many years in the States, and even
though not everything that glitters over there is gold, any
more than here, there's one thing that *is* true, and that is that
one learns to look at things differently and not just through
the same old glass. And one also learns that there are many
paths to grace and many paths to happiness. Yes, Herr Baron,
there are many paths that lead to God, and there are many
paths that lead to happiness; of both these truths I am equally
certain in my heart. And no one path is better than another.
But a path can only be good if it is open, if it is straight, if it
lies full in the sun, if it is free of quagmires, free of swamps,
and free of will-o'-the-wisps. It's a question of veracity, it's a
question of reliability, and it's a question of honesty.'

With these words Franke rose to his feet, and Botho courteously walked him to the door and offered him his hand.

'And now, Herr Franke, one last request before we say
goodbye: give Frau Dörr my regards if you see her and the

old connection is still kept up, and above all give my regards to dear old Frau Nimptsch. Does she still have her gout and her "bad days" that she always used to complain about?'

'That's all over now.'

'How so?'

'We buried her three weeks ago, Herr Baron. Exactly three weeks ago today.'

'Buried her?' repeated Botho. 'And where?'

'Out beyond the Rollkrug, in the New St James' Cemetery ... A fine old lady. And how she doted on her Lene! Yes, Herr Baron, Mother Nimptsch is dead. But Frau Dörr, *she*'s alive all right,' he laughed as he spoke, 'and she'll live a long time yet. Next time she comes by – and it's a long walk – I'll pass on your regards. I can already see how pleased she'll be. You know how she is, Herr Baron. Yes, Frau Dörr ...'

Gideon Franke raised his hat once more, and the door closed behind him.

21

ONCE he was alone again Botho felt quite benumbed by this meeting, and above all by what he had heard at its close. When in the intervening years his thoughts had turned to the little garden-house and its occupants, his mind's eye had naturally pictured everything just as it had been, but now all was changed and he had to find his bearings in a quite new reality. Strangers were living in the little house, if it was inhabited at all, and there was no fire burning in the hearth, at least not day in day out; and Frau Nimptsch, who had tended the fire, was dead and lay out in the St James' Cemetery. As all this washed over his mind he suddenly recalled the day when he had promised the old woman, half solemnly and half in jest, to lay a wreath of immortelles on her grave. In his present

agitated state he was somehow glad that his old pledge had
come back to him, and he resolved to make it good at once.
'To the Rollkrug in the scorching midday sun – almost like
crossing the Sahara. But the kind old soul shall have her
wreath.'

And he immediately took up his sword and cap and started
out.

There was a bay for cabs on the corner, but only a small one,
so that despite the notice that read 'Cab-Rank: Three Spaces',
only very rarely was even a single cab to be found there. It
stood empty again today, which was scarcely surprising given
that it was noon (when cabs everywhere tend to vanish as if
the earth had swallowed them up) and the rank in any case
only really existed in name. So Botho walked on until he saw
a rather rickety, light green vehicle with red plush seats drawn
by a grey coming towards him near the Van der Heydt Bridge.
The grey was moving along so slowly that Botho could not
help smiling ruefully at the thought of the long 'excursion'
the poor beast had ahead of it. But although he looked far and
wide there was nothing better in sight, so he went up to the
driver and said: 'To the Rollkrug. St James' Cemetery.'

'Very good, Herr Baron.'

'... But we'll have to stop on the way. I want to buy a
wreath.'

'Very good, Herr Baron.'

Botho was somewhat surprised at this prompt and repeated
use of his title, and therefore asked, 'Do you know me?'

'Certainly, Herr Baron. Baron Rienäcker, Landgrafenstrasse. Right by the cab-rank. Driven you many a time.'

As they spoke Botho climbed in, intending to make himself
as comfortable as he could in the plush-upholstered corner,
but it was as hot as an oven and he soon gave up the idea.

Like all noblemen from the Mark he possessed the attract-
ive, heart-warming trait of liking to chat with the common
people, far more than with the 'educated' classes, and as they

drove along in the partial shade of the young trees lining the canal he readily started a conversation: 'What a heat! Your grey won't have been too thrilled when he heard me say "Rollkrug".'

'Oh, the Rollkrug ain't too bad. Rollkrug's all right 'cos o' the heathland. When he goes that way the scent o' the pine trees always gives him a lift. He's country-bred, you see ... Or maybe it's the music. Leastways he always pricks his ears up.'

'I see,' said Botho. 'He doesn't look like he'd be up to dancing, though ... But where can we get a wreath? I shouldn't like to arrive at the cemetery without one.'

'Oh, there's plenty o' time for that, Herr Baron, when we get to the cemetery district, from the Halle Gate right the way down the Pionierstrasse.'

'Yes, of course, you're right. I remember now ...'

'An' even after that there's some more, right up to near the cemetery.'

Botho smiled. 'You're Silesian, aren't you?'

'Yes,' said the driver. 'Most of us are. But I've been here a long time an' so really I'm halfway to bein' a proper Berliner.'

'And are you doing well?'

'I wouldn't say "well", no. Everythin' costs so much, an' only the best'll do. An' oats is dear. It'd be all right if nothin' ever went wrong. But somethin' always does – one day an axle breaks, another day a horse tumbles. I've got a chestnut at home that's been in service with the Fürstenwald Lancers; a neat horse, only he ain't got no wind left an' can't go on much longer. So that's him done for. An' then the traffic police – never satisfied, always nigglin' over this or that. Forever at us to repaint the cabs. An' that red plush don't come free neither.'

Chatting as they made their way along the canal, they reached the Halle Gate. An infantry battalion was coming towards them from the direction of Kreuzberg with its band playing lustily, and Botho, who wanted to avoid meeting anyone, pressed the driver to go faster. So they sped past the Belle Alliance Bridge, but on the far side he called for a halt when he read the words 'Florist and Nurseryman' on one of the first houses. Three or four steps led up to a shop with all sorts of wreaths in its large display window.

Rienäcker climbed out and went up the steps. As he entered through the doorway a bell jangled sharply. 'Would you be so kind as to show me a nice wreath, please?'

'For a funeral?'

'Yes.'

Dressed in black, the assistant had in her whole appearance, even down to the shears in her hand, a somewhat ridiculous resemblance to one of the Three Fates, perhaps in consideration of the fact that it was mainly burial wreaths that were sold here. Soon she returned with a myrtle wreath interwoven with white roses. She apologized that they were only white roses, saying that white camellias would have been more the thing. But Botho was quite satisfied and had no objections to make, only asking if he might have a wreath of immortelles to go with this fresh-cut one.

The assistant looked rather surprised at receiving such an old-fashioned request, but replied in the affirmative and presently reappeared with a cardboard box containing five or six immortelle wreaths – yellow, red and white.

'Which colour would you recommend?'

The girl smiled: 'Immortelle wreaths are completely out of fashion. In winter you might just ... And even then only ...'

'This one here will be best.' And with that Botho hung the yellow wreath nearest him over his arm, asked for the other one with myrtle and white roses to be brought out, and then hastened to get back into his cab. Both wreaths were quite big and looked so conspicuous lying on the red-plush rear seat that he wondered if he should not rather hand them to the driver. However he quickly rejected this impulse, saying to himself, 'If you want to bring old Frau Nimptsch a wreath, you must do it openly. If you're too ashamed then you shouldn't have promised in the first place.'

So he left the wreaths where they were, and almost entirely forgot about them soon afterwards as the cab turned into a stretch of road that offered such a colourful, in places grotesque spectacle that he was quite diverted from his previous musings. To the right, running along the road for about five hundred paces, stood a wooden fence, and rising above it on the far side was a jumble of stalls, pavilions and illuminated entrances, all covered with an extraordinary array of signboards. Most of them were recent or even brand new, but the largest and most colourful had a more venerable history as survivals, albeit rather washed out by the rain, of the previous year. Dotted among the stalls in the midst of this fairground various master craftsmen had set up their workshops, predominantly sculptors and stonecutters, and in view of the numerous cemeteries in the area their displays were mainly confined to crosses, columns and obelisks. All this could not fail to make an impression on anyone who passed this way, and Rienäcker was no exception, studying with growing curiosity from his cab the never-ending and crassly contrasting advertising slogans and the images that accompanied them: 'Fräulein Rosella the Girl Prodigy – See Her Live'; 'Gravestones at Unbeatable Prices'; 'American Instant Photography'; 'Russian Cockshy – Six Throws for Ten Pfennigs'; 'Swedish Punch with Waffles'; 'Figaro's Finest Cut – or the World's Best Hair Salon'; 'Gravestones at Unbeatable Prices'; 'Swiss Shooting Gallery:

> 'Aim it fast and aim it well,
> Aim and score like William Tell'

– and underneath Tell himself, complete with crossbow, son and apple.

Finally the fence came to an end, and at this point the

road took a sharp turn towards the Hasen Heath, from which Botho could hear the rat-a-tat of rifles from the shooting ranges in the midday calm. Otherwise this section of the road was much like the one before it. The acrobat Blondin, wearing only a bathing suit and his medals, stood poised on a tightrope amid a blaze of fireworks, while all about him a variety of smaller placards announced everything from balloon ascents to dance entertainments. One of them read: 'Sicilian Night. Viennese Bonbon Waltz at Two o'Clock'.

Botho, who had not been this way for years, read everything with unfeigned interest. After a few minutes he passed beyond the Hasen Heath and the refreshing shade it had afforded and entered the main street of a bustling suburb that extended all the way to Rixdorf.* The vehicles in front were travelling two and three abreast, until suddenly the traffic snarled up and everything came to a standstill. 'Why are we stopping?' But before the driver could answer, Botho heard people scolding and cursing up ahead and saw that several vehicles had got into a tangle. He leant forward and peered out on all sides, and with his characteristic predilection for lower-class life he would most likely have derived more enjoyment than irritation from the whole incident if he had not just then spotted a cart that had come to a stop in front of him, whose inscription, together with the load it was carrying, prompted him to melancholy reflections. 'Max Zippel of Rixdorf. Broken Glass Bought and Sold' was written in large letters on the wall-like tailboard, and the cart was piled high with glass fragments. 'Fortune and glass …'† And he stared at it with a shudder, and his fingertips tingled as if pierced by the fragments.

---

* Village to the south-east of Berlin, which in 1912 sought to cast off its reputation as a place of cheap entertainment by changing its name to Neu-kölln (New Cologne).

† '… soon break, alas!'

Eventually the column of vehicles began moving again. Not only that, but the grey did his best to make up for lost time, and before long the driver stopped at a corner house built on rising ground with a tall roof and projecting gable, its ground-floor windows so low as to be almost on a level with the street. A cast-iron arm reached out from the gable and held a gold-coloured key with its point aloft.

'What's that?' asked Botho.

'The Rollkrug.'

'Good. Then we're almost there. Just up this hill now. I feel sorry for your grey, but there's nothing for it.'

The driver gave the horse a flick of his whip and they began ascending the moderately steep road up the hill. On one side was the Old St James' Cemetery, now over-full and therefore partly closed off, while facing its perimeter fence on the other side of the road tall tenement blocks rose skywards.

Before the last building stood a pair of itinerant musicians playing a horn and a harp, to all appearances man and wife. The woman was singing as well, but the wind, which blew quite sharply here, carried the sound uphill, and Botho could not make out the words and melody until he had passed the poor players by ten paces or more. It was the very song they had so gaily and happily sung all that time ago on the walk back from Wilmersdorf, and, just as if someone had called after him, he got up from his seat and looked back at the musicians. They were facing another way and did not see him, but a pretty housemaid cleaning the windows at the building's gable end must have thought the young officer had turned back to glance at her, so she waved her leather cloth merrily from her window seat and joined in with gusto:

> 'I still remember I owe my life to you,
> But soldier, soldier, do *you* remember too?'

Botho threw himself back in his seat and pressed his hand

to his brow as an infinitely sweet, infinitely painful sensation took hold of him. But the pain was stronger, and it only fell away once the city lay behind him and on the distant horizon the Müggel Hills emerged from the blue midday haze.

At last they drew up in front of the New St James' Cemetery.

'Shall I wait?'

'Yes. But not here. Down by the Rollkrug. And if the musicians are still there . . . here, this is for the poor woman.'

22

BOTHO placed himself under the guidance of an old man working at the entrance of the cemetery and found Frau Nimptsch's grave well tended: twines of ivy had been planted, a potted geranium stood among them, and an immortelle wreath was already hanging from a small iron post. 'Ah, Lene,' said Botho to himself. 'You haven't changed . . . I've come too late.' Then he turned to the old man standing beside him and said, 'Only a small funeral, I suppose.'

'Yes, it was small all right.'

'Three or four?'

'Four exactly. An' o' course our old superintendent.* He jus' said the prayer, an' the big, middle-aged woman who was with 'em, forty or thereabouts, she cried all the way through. And there was a younger one too. She comes every week now, and last Sunday she brought the geranium. She wants to get a stone too, the way people like 'em now: green glaze with the name and dates on.'

At this point the old man withdrew with the professional

---

* In the Lutheran Church a senior pastor supervising the ministry in a church district comprising several parishes.

politeness of all cemetery employees, while Botho attached his immortelle wreath to the one Lene had already brought and placed the one with myrtle and white roses around the geranium pot. Then he contemplated the simple grave awhile and thought of the good Frau Nimptsch with affection before making his way back to the cemetery entrance. The old man, who had now resumed his work on the trellis there, gazed after him and doffed his cap, at the same time mulling over the question of what might have brought such a fine gentleman – and his last handshake had left him in no doubt of this – to the old woman's grave. 'Mus' be somethin' to it. An' didn't make the cab wait neither.' But he came to no conclusion, and wishing at least to show his gratitude as best he could he picked up one of the watering cans standing nearby and went first to the small cast-iron fountain and then over to Frau Nimptsch's grave to water the ivy, which had become rather dry in the burning sun.

Meanwhile Botho walked back to the cab waiting outside the Rollkrug, got in, and an hour later was back in the Landgrafenstrasse. The driver jumped down assiduously and opened the door.

'There you are,' said Botho. 'And here's a bit extra. That really was halfway to being a country outing.'

'More'n halfway, you might say.'

'I see,' said Rienäcker with a laugh. 'So I have to add a bit more.'

'Wouldn't hurt ... Thankin' you kindly, Herr Baron.'

'But now feed that grey up a bit for me. He's a sorry sight.'

And he nodded and went up the steps.

In his apartment everything was quiet. Even the servants were out since they knew that at this hour he was always at his Club, or at least he had been since becoming a grass widower. 'Unreliable people,' he grumbled to himself in apparent annoyance. In fact, though, he was pleased to be alone. He did not wish to see anyone and sat out on the balcony to indulge in his reveries. But the big canvas awning had been lowered and it was stifling underneath, all the more so for the long blue-white fringes hanging from it. He stood to wind it up, and the fresh breeze that now wafted towards him made him feel better. He inhaled deeply as he stepped up to the balustrade and looked out over the fields and woods as far as the Charlottenburg Palace dome, whose malachite-coloured copper plating shimmered in the brilliance of the afternoon sun.

'Beyond there lies Spandau,' he said to himself, 'and beyond that is a railway embankment and a track that runs all the way to the Rhine. And on that track I can see a train with many carriages, and in one of those carriages sits Käthe. I wonder how she looks. Good, I'm sure. And what's she talking about? Well, all sorts of things, I imagine: piquant watering-place anecdotes and maybe Frau Salinger's dresses, and that after all there's nowhere like Berlin. And shouldn't I be glad she's coming back? Such a pretty wife, so young, so happy, so cheerful. And I am glad too. But she mustn't come *today*. Please God, not today. I wouldn't put it past her, though. She hasn't written for three days, and she's a great one for surprises.'

He mused over this a while longer, but then his thoughts took a different turn, and Käthe's image was replaced in his mind by scenes from long ago: the Dörrs' garden, the walk to Wilmersdorf, the trip to Hankel's Stowage. That had been the last perfect day, the last happy moment ... 'She said then that a hair would bind too fast; that's why she refused and wouldn't have it. And I? Why did I insist? Yes, there are mysterious forces like that, strange affinities created by heaven or hell, and now I'm bound and can't break free. Ah, she was so dear and good that afternoon, while we were still alone and had no thought of being disturbed, and I'll never forget the picture of her standing among the tall grasses picking flowers right and left. The flowers – I have them still. But I must have done with them. Why keep these dead things, which only unsettle me and will cost me my little bit of happiness and my domestic peace if anyone else ever spots them?'

He rose from his seat on the balcony and walked the length of the apartment to his study overlooking the courtyard, a bright, sunny room in the mornings but now in deep shade. The coolness did him good, and he went over to an elegant bureau, a relic of his bachelor days, with little ebony drawers inlaid with various tiny silver garlands. In the midst of these drawers was a miniature colonnaded temple with a tympanum for the safekeeping of valuables, towards the back of which was a secret compartment closed with a catch. He now released the catch, and when the compartment sprang open he took out a small bundle of letters tied with a red ribbon. On top of the letters, as if pushed in after them, lay the flowers he had just been thinking about. He weighed the little packet in his hand and murmured, as he untied the ribbon, 'So much joy, so much sorrow. Such tangled paths. An oft-told tale.'

He was alone and could not possibly be taken by surprise, but as he fancied he was still not secure enough he stood up to lock the door. Having done so, he took the uppermost letter and began reading. It was the note she had written the day before the walk to Wilmersdorf, and in rereading it he was moved as his eye was drawn to the words he had marked with a little pencil stroke. 'Garlend ... sooth ... how endearingly they greet me afresh, better than the most perfect spelling in the world! And her handwriting so clear. And what she writes so warm-hearted and mischievous. Ah, she had the best combination of qualities – passion *and* level-headedness. Everything she said showed character and depth of feeling. Educated language, how far it lags behind hers!'

He then took up the second letter with the intention of reading through the whole correspondence in reverse order.

But it hurt too much. 'To what purpose? Why revive and refresh what is dead and must remain so? I must put an end to this, and hope that without these tokens of remembrance the memories themselves will fade away.'

His mind was now made up, and he got up quickly from his bureau, pushed the fire screen to one side, and stepped up to the little fireplace to burn the letters. There he stood, and slowly, as if to prolong the feeling of sweet pain, he let the sheets fall one by one into the hearth to be consumed by the flames. The last thing left in his hand was the posy, and as he pondered and brooded he felt a momentary urge to take a last look at each flower and so untie the strand of hair. But suddenly a superstitious fear seemed to take hold of him, and he threw the posy after the letters.

The flames flickered up, briefly, and then the glow ceased; all was gone.

'Am I free now? ... Do I even want to be? No, I do *not*. Nothing but ashes. And yet still I am bound.'

23

Botho gazed into the ashes. 'So little and yet so much.' He then pushed back the elegant fire screen, which at its centre had a figure reproduced from a Pompeiian mural. His eye had brushed over it a hundred times without observing what it was, but now he saw it properly. 'Minerva with shield and spear,' he said to himself. 'But the spear at her feet. Perhaps it signifies peace ... Would that it did.' Then he stood up, shut the secret compartment, now bereft of its most precious treasure, and made his way back to the front of the apartment.

On his way through the long, narrow corridor he encountered the cook and the maid, who had just that moment returned from a walk in the Tiergarten. At the sight of them standing there, all afraid and confused, he felt an impulse of compassion, but he restrained it and told himself, albeit with a touch of irony, that it was high time he put his foot down. So he began as best he could to play the part of Thundering Zeus. Where on earth had they been? Was this their idea of propriety and good order? When their mistress came back (which she might do today) he didn't want her to find a household in disarray. And what about his batman? 'All right, I don't want to know, nor do I want to hear anything, least of all excuses.' Once he had delivered himself of this he walked on and smiled, chiefly at himself. 'How easy it is to preach, and how much harder to act accordingly! I'm a mere pulpit paragon. For am I not in disarray myself? Where are my propriety and good order? It would be one thing if it were all in the past; what is so bad is that it hasn't ended yet.'

Botho went back to his seat on the balcony and rang the bell. Now it was his batman who appeared, more afraid and confused almost than the two girls; but there was no need, the storm had passed. 'Tell the cook I want something to eat. Well, what are you waiting for? Oh, I see,' and he laughed, 'nothing in the house. Isn't that just splendid ... All right then, tea; bring me some tea – we've got that I hope. And have her make a couple of open sandwiches for me. I'm hungry, for heaven's sake! ... And have the evening papers come?'

'Yes, Herr Rittmeister.'[*]

Before long the tea things were laid on the balcony, and even a bite to eat had been contrived. Botho leant back in the rocking chair and contemplated the small blue flame. Then he picked up his little wife's guiding light the *Fremdenblatt*, and after that the *Kreuzzeitung*, turning to its last page. 'Heavens, how delighted Käthe will be to be able to pore over this last page at source again, in other words twelve hours earlier than in Schlangenbad. And isn't she quite right? "Adalbert von

---

[*] Captain of Horse. Botho has been promoted since his marriage.

Lichterloh, Junior Administrative Officer and Lieutenant in the Reserves, and Hildegard von Lichterloh, née Holtze, are honoured to announce their marriage celebrated this day."[*] Wonderful! No doubt about it: it really does you good to see how life continues its merry course. Weddings and christenings, and a few deaths in between – well, you don't have to read those. Käthe doesn't, and nor do I, except if the Vandals have lost one of their "old gentlemen" and I see the fraternity insignia printed in the death notices. Those I do read, they always amuse me, and I can almost imagine the old fraternity boy stopping off at the tavern on his way to Valhalla – for his last rites, so to speak.'

Hearing the doorbell ring, he put the paper aside. 'Could she really ...?' No, it was nothing, just a subscription list for a soup kitchen sent up by the landlord, on which only fifty pfennigs had been entered. All the same he remained agitated all evening because the possibility that she would surprise him hovered in his mind, and each time he saw a cab turn into the Landgrafenstrasse with a trunk strapped to the front and a lady's travelling hat behind he jumped and told himself, 'There she is; she loves that sort of thing, and I can already hear her saying, "I thought it would be just too comical, Botho!"'

Käthe did not come. Instead a letter arrived the next morning announcing her return in three days' time. She would, she said, travel with Frau Salinger again, who all in all really was a very nice woman – very good-humoured, very chic, and she knew how to travel in style.

Botho put down the letter and at once felt genuinely pleased that he would be seeing his lovely young wife again within three days. 'Our hearts have room for all sorts of

---

[*] Fontane has a Dickensian penchant for comical names, especially in combination. Here the bride's name means 'wood', the groom's 'ablaze'.

contradictions ... She's silly, yes, but a silly young wife is better than none at all.'

Then he called his servants together and informed them that their mistress would be back in three days. They were to put everything to rights and polish the brass. And not a speck of fly dirt on the large mirror.

Having seen to all this he went to perform his duties at the barracks. 'If anyone asks, I'll be at home again from five.'

His programme for the intervening time was that he would remain at the barracks yard until noon, ride for a few hours, and then eat at his Club. There he was sure to find Balafré even if no one else, which meant a game of two-handed whist and a profusion of court gossip, true and false. Reliable source of information though he otherwise was, Balafré made it a principle to set aside an hour each day for nonsense and tall stories. Indeed he enjoyed this pastime, which amounted to a kind of intellectual sport, more than any other.

Botho carried out his programme just as he had devised it. The clock in the barracks yard was just striking twelve as he swung into his saddle, and after making his way along Unter den Linden and down the Luisenstrasse he turned into a path that ran for a stretch next to the canal and then continued its course in the direction of Lake Plötzen. He recalled the day on which he had ridden around this same area trying to summon up the courage to part from Lene, a parting that was so hard and yet had to be. That was three years ago now. How had his life been since? There had been many joys, to be sure. But real, settled happiness had not been his. A sugared plum, not much more, and who can live on sweets alone?

He was still immersed in these thoughts when he spotted two fellow officers approaching on a bridle path that led from the Jungfern Heath to the canal. They were lancers, easy to recognize even from afar by their flat-topped helmets. But who were they? This too soon became clear, for at about a hundred paces Botho identified the oncoming riders as the

Rexins, two cousins serving in the same regiment.

'Ah, Rienäcker,' said the elder. 'Where are you going?'

'Into the blue yonder.'

'That's too far for me.'

'Well, to Saatwinkel then.'

'That's more like it. I'll join you in that case, as long as I'm not intruding ... Kurt,' and he turned to his younger companion, 'forgive me, but I have something to discuss with Rienäcker, and in the circumstances ...'

'... you'd prefer a tête-à-tête. Just as you wish, Bozel.'* And with that Kurt von Rexin saluted and rode on, while the cousin he had addressed turned his horse around and moved to the left of Rienäcker, who stood well above him in the army list. 'Well,' he said, 'Saatwinkel it is, then. I assume we won't be crossing the line of fire at Tegel.'

'I'll certainly do my best to avoid it,' replied Rienäcker, 'firstly for my own sake, and secondly for yours. And thirdly and lastly for Henriette's. What would the raven-haired Henriette say if her Bogislaw were killed, and by a friendly shell to boot?'

'It would certainly give her a pang,' Rexin responded, 'and upset her applecart and mine too.'

'What applecart?'

'That's the very point I wanted to discuss with you, Rienäcker.'

'With me? What point is that?'

'You really ought to be able to guess. It isn't hard. I'm naturally referring to a personal relationship, my own to be precise.'

'Personal relationship!' Botho laughed. 'Well, I'm at your service, Rexin, but I must confess I can't imagine what makes you choose *me* to confide in. I'm no font of wisdom on any subject, least of all that one. We've got much better authori-

---

* Affectionate contraction of Bogislaw.

ties in that field. One of them you know well; indeed he's a particular friend of yours and your cousin's.'

'Balafré?'

'Yes.'

Rexin sensed a certain cool dismissiveness in these words and fell into a rather disgruntled silence. But Botho had not sought this reaction, and immediately softened. 'Forgive me, Rexin. Relationships – there are so very many of them.'

'Yes, so many, and so different.'

Botho shrugged his shoulders and smiled. However Rexin, clearly unwilling to let his sensitivity get the better of him a second time, merely repeated in an equable tone, 'Yes, so many, and so different. And I'm surprised, Rienäcker, to see you of all people shrug your shoulders. I'd have thought ...'

'Well, out with it then.'

'I shall.'

After a few moments Rexin went on, 'I've had an elite training in these matters with the lancers, and also before that (as you know I joined late) at university in Bonn and Göttingen, so I don't need any lessons or advice regarding the common run of things. But if I ask myself honestly, I have to say that my case isn't in the common run; it's an exception.'

'That's what everyone thinks.'

'In short I feel committed. More than that, I love Henriette, or, to give you a better idea of my state of mind, I love my raven-haired Jette. You see, I prefer to use this trite, rather dubious pet name, with its overtones of the canteen, because I want to avoid all airs and solemnity in speaking about this. I'm serious enough as it is, and because I'm serious I've no use for anything that looks like solemnity or flowery language. All that just diminishes it.'

Botho nodded in agreement, and slowly shed the touch of superior mockery he had undoubtedly been displaying.

'Jette,' Rexin continued, 'doesn't spring from a line of angels, and isn't one herself. But then, where are they to be

found? In our circle? Absurd. All these distinctions are arti-
ficial, and nowhere more so than in the case of virtue. I don't
deny that virtue and other fine things exist, but innocence
and virtue are like Bismarck and Moltke, in other words rare.
Over the years I've become completely confirmed in these
views; I feel sure they are right and intend as far as I can to act
accordingly. I tell you, Rienäcker, if instead of riding along
this dreary canal here, as dreary and unbending as the norms
and conventions of our society; if instead of this miserable
ditch we had the Sacramento alongside us, with the Diggings
up ahead rather than the Tegel Shooting Range, I'd marry
Jette right away. I can't live without her; she's captivated
me, and with her naturalness, simplicity and true love she's
worth more than ten countesses to me. But it's no good. I
can't do it to my parents, nor do I wish to leave the service at
twenty-seven to become a cowboy in Texas or a waiter on a
Mississippi steamer. That leaves a middle course ...'

'What do you mean by that?'

'An unsanctioned union.'

'A marriage without a wedding, then.'

'Yes, if you like. The word itself means nothing to me, no
more than legalization, consecration, or whatever the rest
of these things are all called. I've got a nihilist streak in me
and don't set any real store by priestly sanctification. But,
just to say this quickly as well, I do want monogamy; for me
there's no other way, not on moral grounds, but because of
my own inborn nature. I abhor the type of relationship that's
made and broken in the space of an hour, so to speak, and if
I called myself a nihilist just now, I might with even more
reason call myself a philistine. I yearn for simple ways, for a
quiet, natural existence where you can speak heart to heart
and enjoy the best that life has to offer: honesty, love and
freedom.'

'Freedom,' repeated Botho.

'Yes, Rienäcker. But I know that there are dangers lurking

there, and that this happiness in being free – maybe freedom of any kind – is a double-edged sword, and there's no way of knowing which way it will cut. And that's why I wanted to ask what you think.'

'And I shall tell you,' said Rienäcker, who had grown more serious with each minute as the other's confidences undoubtedly put him in mind of his own life, both past and present. 'Yes, Rexin, I shall tell you as best I can, for I believe I'm in a position to do so. And so I implore you, don't go ahead. What you intend can have only two possible outcomes, one as bad as the other. If you take the path of unswerving loyalty, if in other words you break with class, custom and tradition, then your life, even if you don't go to the dogs, will sooner or later become a torment and a burden to you. If, however, after a lengthy period you go back and make peace with society and your family, which is generally what happens, then you face a wretched future, because then you must sever a bond that ties you fast to another person, a bond formed in times of happiness, and indeed even more importantly in times of trouble, hardship and anxiety. And that hurts.'

Rexin seemed about to answer, but Botho did not notice and went on, 'My dear Rexin, you spoke just now with truly masterly restraint of relationships that are "made and broken in the space of an hour". But relationships like this, which hardly deserve the name, are not the worst. The worst are those, to quote you again, which take the "middle course". I'm warning you: beware of this middle course, beware of half-measures. What looks to you like gain is really ruin, and the imagined safe haven will wreck your ship. It *never* turns out well, even if outwardly everything passes off smoothly without any harsh words and barely a hint of reproach. Nor can it be otherwise, for every action has its natural consequences – we must always bear that in mind. What's done cannot be undone, and a picture etched on our minds will never wholly dissolve, never wholly fade away. Memories will remain and comparisons arise. And so once again, my friend, give up this idea, or your life will fall under a cloud and you'll never be able to fight your way back to sunlight and clarity. Many things are permissible, but not what does violence to the soul or entangles the heart, even if it's only your own.'

24

THE THIRD DAY brought a telegram that Käthe had sent at the moment of departure: 'Arriving this evening. K.'

And arrive she did. Botho waited for her at Anhalt Station and was introduced to Frau Salinger, who responded to her thanks for being such a good travel companion with repeated, Viennese-accented assurances that the pleasure had all been *hers*, and above all how happy *he* must be to have such a charming young wife. 'Now I must tell you, Herr Baron, if I had the good fortune of being the husband of a woman like *her*, why, I wouldn't be parted from her even for three days.' And she launched into lamentations about the male sex in general, followed a second later by a pressing invitation to Vienna. 'We've got a cosy little house less than an hour from Vienna with a few saddle horses and a good kitchen. In Prussia you've got the best schools, and in Vienna we've got the best cooking. I'm sure I don't know which I prefer.'

'I know,' said Käthe, 'and I think Botho does too.'

With that they parted, and, after giving instructions to send the luggage on, our young couple climbed into an open carriage. Käthe threw herself back and planted one little foot against the opposite seat, on which lay an enormous bouquet, the last tribute of the landlady in Schlangenbad who had been utterly enchanted by the charming lady from Berlin. Käthe took Botho's arm and nestled up to him, but only for a few seconds, then sat upright again and used her parasol to pin down the bouquet, which kept falling to the floor. As she did so she said, 'It really is delightful here, all the people everywhere, and so many Spree flatboats they've hardly got room to move. And so little dust. I think it's a real blessing that they sprinkle the roads nowadays and drench everything with water; though of course it means you can't wear long dresses. And look at that baker's cart with the dog pulling it. It really is too comical! If only the canal ... I don't know, it's still just so ...'

'Yes,' and Botho laughed. 'It's still just so. Four weeks of July heat haven't done anything to improve it.'

As they passed under some young trees Käthe tore off a linden leaf, placed it in her hollow palm, and slapped it to make a popping noise. 'That's what we always used to do at home. And in Schlangenbad when there was nothing better to do, we went back to all our childhood games there. Just imagine, I'm quite seriously attached to such follies even though I'm an old lady who's done with the world.'

'Käthe, really!'

'Yes, yes, a real matron, you'll see ... But look, Botho, that palisade's still there and the old wheat beer tavern with its comical and rather rude name* that we found so frightfully funny as schoolgirls. I thought it would have closed ages ago. But the Berliners won't let something like that be taken from them, and so it stays put. They like anything as long as it's got a queer name they can laugh at.'

Botho did not quite know whether he was feeling happy or slightly disgruntled. 'I see you haven't changed a bit, Käthe.'

'Of course not. Why should I? I wasn't sent to Schlangenbad to change, at least not in my character or conversation. As to whether I've changed in any other way, well *cher ami, nous*

---

* Well-known tavern on the Tempelhofer Ufer named after its first owner Buberitz, whose name was deliberately mispronounced as Puperitz ('Fart-Crack').

verrons.'

'A matron?'

She put her finger to his mouth and tossed back the veil of her travelling hat, which had half fallen over her face. A moment later they passed under the Potsdam railway viaduct, just as an express train was roaring across the iron girders above. Everything shook and thundered, and once they emerged on the other side Käthe said, 'It always gives me a turn being right underneath like that.'

'It's no better for the people on top.'

'Maybe not. But it's a question of perception. Perceptions are so powerful, don't you think?' And she sighed as if something horrifying had penetrated her life and suddenly revealed itself to her. But then she said, 'In England, so Mr Armstrong told me – he was someone I met at Schlangenbad, I must tell you all about him; married to an Alvensleben, incidentally – anyway, he said that in England they bury the dead fifteen feet deep. Now, fifteen feet is no worse than five, but when he said it I could positively feel the "clay" (that's the correct English word) pressing down like a ton weight on my chest. Because in England they've got heavy clay soil.'

'Armstrong, you say … There was an Armstrong in the Baden Dragoons.'

'A cousin of his. They're all cousins, just like with us. I can't wait to describe him to you with all his little peculiarities. A perfect gentleman with upturned moustaches, although he did take somewhat exaggerated care of them. They looked very comical, those twirled points, which he was always twirling even tighter.'

Ten minutes later their carriage pulled up outside their apartment, and Botho gave her his arm and led her up the steps. There was a garland decorating the big door to the corridor, and hanging slightly askew from it a sign with the word *Willkommen*, from which one *l* was unfortunately missing. Käthe looked up and laughed as she read it.

'"Welcome"! But with only one *l*, so only half meant. Oh dear! And *l* is for "love" too. Oh, well. I suppose I'm only to have half of everything.'

With that she stepped through into the corridor, where the cook and the maid stood waiting to kiss her hand.

'Hello, Berta. Hello, Minette. Yes, my little friends, here I am again. Well, what do you think? Am I looking better?' And before the girls had time to reply – not that a reply was called for – she continued, '*You're* certainly looking better, anyway. Especially you, Minette; you've really filled out.'

Minette looked down in embarrassment, and so Käthe added good-naturedly, 'I mean, just here around your chin and neck.'

Meanwhile the batman appeared too. 'Well, Orth, I was getting worried about you. Quite needlessly, I'm glad to see. None the worse for wear, except you're a trifle pale. But that'll just be the heat. And still the same freckles.'

'Yes, gracious lady, there's no shiftin' *them*.'

'Quite right too. Stick to your true colours.'

Amid these exchanges she got as far as her bedroom with Botho and Minette following, while the other two withdrew to their usual haunts in the kitchen area.

'Now, Minette, come and help me. First my coat. And now my hat, but be careful taking it off or we'll have dust every-where. And now tell Orth to lay the table out on the balcony. I haven't touched a morsel all day because I wanted to make the most of eating here among you all. Now off you go, my pet. Quickly, Minette.'

Minette hurriedly finished her operations and went out, while Käthe stood before the cheval mirror and tidied her disordered hair. At the same time she glanced at Botho's reflection as he stood close by with his eyes fixed on his beau-tiful young wife.

'Well, Botho,' she said in a mischievous, coquettish tone without looking round.

Her winsome coquetry did not miss its target. He embraced her, and she yielded to his caresses. Then he encircled her waist and swept her up in the air. 'Käthe, my doll, my sweet little doll!'

'Sweet little doll! I ought to be cross with you for that, Botho. Dolls are for playing with. But I'm not cross – on the contrary. Dolls are loved the most and treated the best. And that's what counts with me.'

25

IT WAS a glorious morning, with the sky partially clouded over and a gentle westerly breeze. The young husband and wife sat on the balcony, and as Minette cleared away the coffee things they looked across at the Zoological Gardens, where the brightly-coloured domes of the Elephant Houses were glinting in the morning haze.

'I still don't really know a thing,' said Botho. 'You went straight to sleep, and sleep is sacred to me. But now I want to know all about it. So tell me.'

'Tell you – yes, but what? I've written you so many letters, and by now you must be as familiar with Anna Grävenitz and Frau Salinger as I am, or maybe more so, because now and then I said more than I actually knew.'

'Indeed. But just as often you wrote "More when we meet". Well, now's the moment, or else I'll think you've got something to hide. I know nothing whatever of your excursions, and you were in Wiesbaden, weren't you? People say Wiesbaden is full of old colonels and generals, but there are Englishmen too. And that reminds me of the Scotsman you were going to tell me about. What was his name again?'

'Armstrong. Mr Armstrong. Yes, he was a delightful man, and I could never understand his wife – an Alvensleben, as I think I've already said – who got embarrassed every time he spoke. He really was a perfect gentleman, very particular in his manners even when he let himself go rather and indulged in a kind of nonchalance. It's at moments like those that you can always tell a true gentleman, don't you think? He wore a blue necktie and a yellow summer suit that looked as if it had been sewn onto him, and so Anna Grävenitz would always say, 'Here comes the pen-holder'. And outdoors he always carried a large open parasol, a habit he'd picked up in India. You see he was an officer in a Scottish regiment that had done a long stint in Madras or Bombay, or was it Delhi? It makes no difference. What a life he'd led! His conversation was charming, though at times it was hard to know how to take it.'

'You mean he was forward, insolent?'

'Really, Botho, what are you saying? A man like him, a gentleman *comme il faut*. Well, I'll give you an example of the sort of thing he said. One day we were sitting opposite old Frau von Wedell, the general's wife, and Anna Grävenitz asked (I think it was the anniversary of Königgrätz)[*] if it was really true that thirty-three Wedells had fallen in the Seven Years' War. Frau von Wedell said it was, and added that the real figure was in fact a little higher. This astonished everyone sitting nearby except for Mr Armstrong, and when I jokingly took him to task for being so unmoved he said he couldn't get excited at such small numbers. "Small numbers!" I exclaimed, but he just laughed and then turned my point against me by saying that a hundred and thirty-three Armstrongs had been killed in various wars and clan feuds. At first Frau von Wedell wouldn't believe it, but when Mr Armstrong stuck to his guns she asked with great curiosity if all hundred and thirty-three had really "fallen", and he said, "No, my gracious lady, not exactly fallen; most of them were hanged for horse-thieving

---

* Also known as the Battle of Sadowa, the decisive victory of Prussian over Austrian arms in the war of 1866.

by the English, our enemies at the time." Everyone was
scandalized at this unseemly, indeed one might say rather
shocking way of meeting one's end, but he insisted we were
quite wrong to take exception to it, for times change and so do
people's attitudes, and as for his own family, which was after
all intimately concerned in the matter, they looked back with
pride upon these heroic forebears. For three hundred years
cattle- and horse-thieving had been the Scottish way of war, a
simple national custom, and he personally couldn't see much
difference between stealing cattle and stealing countries.'

'A Guelph* in disguise!' said Botho. 'Still, he's got a point.'

'Of course he has. And I always took his part when he
came out with statements like that. Oh, he really was hilar-
ious! He said one shouldn't be too solemn about anything,
it wasn't worth it, and the only serious pursuit in life was
fishing. Sometimes he spends a full fortnight fishing on Loch
Ness or Loch Lochy – you can't imagine the comical names
they have in Scotland! – and then he sleeps on the boat and is
up and doing every morning at sunrise, and at the end of the
fortnight he moults and a whole layer of scaly skin comes off
and leaves him with a new skin like a baby's. And he says he
does it all out of vanity, because a smooth, clear complexion
is the best thing anyone can possess. And as he said that he
looked at me in such a way that for a second I was at a loss
for an answer. Really, you men! But it's a fact that I felt a real
bond with him from the start and didn't object to his manner
of speaking, which sometimes involved him going into great
detail about something, though much, much more often he
would flit from one thing to the next. One of his mottoes was:
"I hate it when a single dish stays on the table for an hour;
change is the great thing, and I'm much happier when the
dishes keep being replaced." And that's how he was, always

---

* A parallel between an earlier Scotland and the Hanover of the 1870s, both
bitterly opposed to domination by a more powerful neighbour.

going helter-skelter through a hundred different topics.'

'Well, in that case you must have got on like a house on fire,' said Botho, laughing.

'We did indeed. And we mean to write each other letters in exactly the style we used in talking; we agreed on that when we said goodbye. Our men, including your friends, are always so thorough. And you're the most thorough of all, which sometimes really depresses me and makes me impatient. You must promise to be more like Mr Armstrong and go in for a bit of simple, harmless chat, and be a bit brisker about it and not always stick to the same subject.'

Botho promised to reform, and Käthe, who loved superlatives, went on to portray a phenomenally rich American, a completely albino Swede with rabbit eyes, and a fascinating Spanish beauty, and then gave him an account of an afternoon excursion to Limburg, Oranienstein and Nassau, describing in turn the crypt, the officer cadet school and the hydropathic institute, before suddenly pointing to the Charlottenburg Palace dome and saying, 'You know, Botho, we really must go there today, or else to Westend or Halensee. The Berlin air is rather stifling, not a bit like the breath of God that wafts abroad and poets so rightly praise. And when you've come fresh from the lap of nature, as I have, you have a renewed affection for what I might call innocence and purity. Ah, Botho, an innocent heart is such a precious thing! I've made a firm resolve to keep my heart pure. And you must help me – indeed you must. Promise? No, not like that; you must kiss me three times on the forehead, like a bride. I don't want any caresses, I want a kiss of consecration ... And if we make do with a light lunch, something warm of course, we can be out there by three.'

Drive out they did, and although the air at Charlottenburg was even further removed from the 'Breath of God' than that of Berlin Käthe made up her mind to remain in the palace

gardens and drop the idea of Halensee. Westend was so
dull, she said, and getting to Halensee took ages, almost like
travelling back to Schlangenbad, but in the palace gardens
you could see the mausoleum with its blue lighting that was
always so strangely moving – like a piece of Heaven dropping
into your soul, you might say. It put you in a devotional mood
and gave you religious thoughts. And even if the mausoleum
hadn't been there, there was always the bridge over the carp
pond with its little bell, and every time a big, mossy old carp
came along she thought it must be a crocodile. And perhaps
there would be a woman there selling biscuits and wafer
cakes, so that they could perform a minor good work by
buying something from her. She chose the words 'good work'
deliberately and avoided 'Christian', she said, because Frau
Salinger had always been charitable like that too.

They followed their plan, and after feeding the carp they
walked further on in the gardens until they came to the
Belvedere with its rococo figures and its historical associa-
tions. Käthe knew nothing of these, so Botho took the opportunity of telling her how on this very spot General von
Bischofswerder had summoned up the ghosts of departed
emperors and electoral princes in an attempt to pull King
Frederick William II out of his lethargy, or, to put it another
way, rescue him from his mistress's grip and lead him back to
the path of virtue.

'And did it do any good?' asked Käthe.

'No.'

'Pity. I always find stories like that so very upsetting. And
it makes my heart bleed to think that the unhappy king (for
he *must* have been unhappy) was the father-in-law of Queen
Louise.* How she must have suffered! I can hardly imagine

---

* Prussia's most romantic queen; famous for her beauty, the love she inspired in her husband Frederick William III (ruled 1797-1840), and her
courage and dignity during the Napoleonic Wars.

how such things can have gone on in our dear old Prussia. And the general who summoned up the ghosts was called Bischofswerder, you say?'

'Yes. At court he was known as Tree Frog.'*

'Because he could forecast the weather?'

'No, because he wore a green coat.'

'Oh, that's too comical ... Tree Frog!'

26

AT SUNDOWN they were back home, and after handing her hat and coat to Minette and ordering their tea Käthe followed Botho into his study, for she needed the satisfaction of knowing that she had spent the first day after her return entirely at his side.

Botho was content to have her with him, and because she was feeling chilly he slid a cushion under her feet and wrapped a blanket over her. Presently, however, he was called away to attend briefly to an urgent item of army business.

Minutes passed, and as the cushion and blanket did not give her as much warmth as she desired Käthe rang the bell and asked the servant who appeared to fetch a few pieces of wood. She was so cold, she said.

At the same time she got up to move the fire screen aside, and as she did so she saw the little heap of ash still lying in the iron grate.

Just then Botho came back into the room and gave a start at the sight before his eyes. But he immediately collected

---

* It was an old custom to keep a tree frog in a glass bowl half-filled with water and fitted with a tiny ladder. Accordingly as good or bad weather approached the frog would climb out of the water or descend back into it. The term *Wetterfrosch* (weather frog) is still applied to someone given to forecasting the weather.

himself when Käthe pointed to the ashes and asked in her most jocular tone, 'What's all this, Botho? See, I've caught you out again. Now confess! Love letters, yes or no?'

'You must think what you please.'

'Yes or no?'

'Very well, yes.'

'*That* was right of you. Now I can be easy. Love letters, how comical! But we'd better burn them twice – first to ashes, then to smoke. Perhaps it will work.'

Deftly she arranged the pieces of wood the servant had meanwhile brought in and tried to kindle them with a few matches. She succeeded, for in an instant the fire was burning brightly. Then she pushed the armchair closer to the blaze, warmed her feet by stretching them snugly right up to the iron bars, and began, 'And now I'll tell you the whole story of the Russian woman, who naturally wasn't Russian at all. A very clever creature, though. She had almond eyes – women like that all have almond eyes – and claimed to be in Schlangenbad for the waters. Well, she was bound to say that. She had no doctor, at least not a proper one, but every day she'd be off to Frankfurt or Wiesbaden, or sometimes Darmstadt, always with a gentleman friend. Not even the same one each time, some people said. And you should have seen the dresses she wore and the airs she gave herself! She gave the barest of greetings when she arrived in the dining room with her maid of honour. And she really had a maid of honour; that's always a first principle with ladies of that sort. We called her "La Pompadour" – the Russian woman, I mean – and she knew that was our name for her. Anyway, one day old Frau von Wedell, who was completely on our side and quite put out by the dubious creature (and a "creature" she was, no doubt about that) – Frau von Wedell said quite loudly across the table, "Yes, ladies, fashions change in everything, even in bags, handbags and purses. When I was a girl we had what we called 'pompadours', but you don't see them any more. No, I really don't believe you see pompadours any more." And we all laughed and looked at La Pompadour. But the dreadful creature got the better of us all the same, for she replied in a loud and penetrating voice (the old lady being a little deaf), "Yes, Frau von Wedell, it is as you say. But the curious thing is that when pompadours fell from favour they were replaced by 'réticules', which later became known as 'ridicules', and some of these 'ridicules' are still with us today." And she looked straight at dear old Frau von Wedell, who couldn't think of an answer and had to get up and leave the room. Now what do you say to that, I ask you? What do you say to such impudence? . . . But Botho, why don't you say something. You're not even listening . . .'

'I am, Käthe, I am.'

Three weeks later there was a wedding in St James's Church, and as always on such occasions its cloister-like porch was densely packed with curious onlookers, mainly working-class women, some with infants in their arms. Schoolchildren and street urchins had congregated too. Various carriages drew up, and from one of the first a couple emerged, to be met with laughter and muffled comments that lasted for as long as they remained visible.

'What a waistline!' said one of the women standing nearby.

'Waistline?'

'Well, hips then.'

'Whalebone, more like.'

'*That*'s true.'

This exchange would doubtless have continued but for the arrival that moment of the bridal carriage. The coachman sprang down from the box and hurried round to open the door, but the bridegroom himself, a gaunt man wearing a tall hat and pointed stand-up collars, got there before him and handed his bride out. She was a very pretty girl, but like most brides won more admiration for her white satin dress than

for her good looks. Together they went up the short flight
of stone steps, laid with a somewhat threadbare carpet, and
entered first the cloistered porch and then the church portal.
All eyes were upon them.

'No bridal wreath!' said the woman before whose critical
eyes Frau Dörr's waistline had just now fared so poorly.

'Bridal wreath indeed! ... Didn't you know? ... Haven't
you heard what they're saying?'

'Oh, I see. Yes, 'course I have. But Frau Kornatzki, my
dear, if everyone went by rumours there'd be no more wreaths
at all, and Schmidt's in the Friedrichstrasse might as well
shut up shop.'

'Yes, yes,' Frau Kornatzki laughed, 'he could an' all. An'
then such an old 'un she's marryin'! Must be fifty if he's a
day, an' looked all set to celebrate his silver at the same time.'

'Yes, he did too. And did you see them pointed collars?
Seems almost unreal.'

'He can use 'em to do her in if there's any more rumours.'

'You're right, he can.'

And so their conversation ran on for a few moments more,
while from inside the church came the opening strains of the
organ prelude.

The following morning the Rienäckers were sitting at
breakfast, this time in Botho's study, where both windows
stood wide open to admit air and light. Swallows nesting
around the courtyard twittered as they flew by, and Botho, in
the habit of scattering some crumbs for them each morning,
was just picking up the breadbasket when a peal of laughter
from his young wife, who for the past five minutes had been
engrossed in her favourite paper, made him set it down again.

'Well, Käthe, what is it? You seem to have found a particularly tasty morsel.'

'I certainly have ... It's simply too comical, the names
there are! Especially in wedding and engagement notices. Just

listen to this.'

'I'm all ears.'

'"Gideon Franke, factory foreman, and Magdalene Franke, née Nimptsch, respectfully announce their marriage celebrated on this day." Nimptsch! Have you ever heard anything more comical? And then Gideon!'

Botho took the paper, though only because he wanted to conceal his embarrassment behind it. Then he handed it back, and in as light a tone as he could muster said, 'But what have you got against Gideon, Käthe? Gideon's better than Botho.'

Afterword

ONE OF THE ODDEST THINGS about Theodor Fontane's career as a novelist is how late it began. He was approaching sixty when his first novel appeared in 1878, two years after he gave up his post with the Academy of Arts in Berlin to devote himself to his chosen vocation. 'I am just starting,' he told his publisher with pride and trepidation. 'Everything lies ahead of me, nothing behind me.'[1] With theatre-reviewing providing his only steady stream of income, and under the perplexed gaze of his wife, who doubted his literary talent and struggled to forgive him for throwing up a well-paid job, he spent the next twenty years producing novels, among them some of the most enduringly popular in the German language.

Fontane was born on 30 December 1819 in Neuruppin, a garrison town north-west of Berlin, the son of a pharmacist and descended through both parents from the French Huguenot refugees who had settled in Prussia in the late seventeenth century. He attended schools in Neuruppin and Swinemünde, the small town on the Baltic coast to which the family moved a few years later, but his most important teacher was his charming, eccentric, rather unsteady father, who spent hours questioning him on the lives of great men and enacting historical anecdotes with him – what he called his 'Socratic method', which gave the boy a lifelong passion for character and dialogue. Three years at a vocational school in Berlin completed his formal education at the age of sixteen, after which he too trained as a pharmacist. On completing his apprenticeship he worked as a journeyman in various towns, but was always keener on writing poetry and translating English authors (having learnt the language by reading it) than on his tasks at the shop counter. He joined literary clubs, where some of his efforts got their first airing. His first publications were two volumes of ballads, which appeared soon after he decided, in 1849, to put aside his pestle and mortar for good.

In 1850 he married Emilie Rouanet-Kummer, like him of Huguenot stock. As a husband, and soon a father, he needed secure employment, and found it in Berlin as a journalist in the pay of the government press office. He had previously inclined towards the republican cause, and the events of 1848 found him on the barricades, so it was with some misgivings that he undertook his new duties. But his association with the government, which took various guises in the following years, benefited him when he was sent to England for several months in 1852 and several years in 1855 to write articles on Anglo-Prussian affairs for home consumption and plant copy favourable to Prussia in the British press. During these sojourns he deepened a long-standing interest in his host nation's literature, then much in vogue in Germany. Among novelists he particularly treasured Scott, Thackeray, Dickens and Charlotte Brontë, and in later years he acquainted himself with George Eliot and the eighteenth-century humorists Fielding, Sterne and Smollett.

Before returning to Berlin in 1859 Fontane went on a tour of Scotland, vividly recorded in his *Jenseit des Tweed* (*Beyond the Tweed*), and under this stimulus he began a regional and historical description of his native Brandenburg, loosely structured as a travelogue and filled with colourful anecdotes. This became his main project of the 1860s and an intermittent preoccupation thereafter, appearing as a series of volumes collectively entitled *Wanderungen durch die*

Mark Brandenburg (*Rambles through Brandenburg*). It was an unlikely idea, for there seemed little romance in the flat landscapes, scanty cultural achievements and earthbound people of this Prussian heartland, but he produced a fine evocation of the region and its sturdy traditions that still finds appreciative readers today. During this time he also worked as a journalist for the *Kreuzzeitung*, the paper of the landed interest, and was commissioned to write long accounts of Prussia's wars of 1864 against Denmark, 1866 against Austria, and 1870-71 against France.

German unification, the goal and outcome of these feats of arms, marks the beginning of a shift in Fontane's political outlook. After two decades working for official press organs and for a paper whose motto was 'With God for King and Country', the former revolutionary had come to be seen, and to see himself, as a conservative. But though he rejoiced in national unity he soon grew disenchanted with many aspects of the new Reich. The brash materialism of the newly-rich middle classes and strutting militarism of the officer corps particularly galled him, as, increasingly, did the narrow selfishness of the old Junker families. Only the working classes held promise for the future, he believed, and could not be denied their just deserts for much longer.

Heralding this shift, Fontane left the *Kreuzzeitung* in 1870 to work as a theatre critic for the liberal *Vossische Zeitung*. For the next nineteen years he wrote pithy, often humorous reviews, which, like his longer essays on novelists such as Freytag, Raabe, Pérez Galdós, Turgenev and Zola, belie acute critical powers with an easy-going, homely style. In 1876 he was appointed first secretary of the Academy of Arts in Berlin, but soon realized that he had no aptitude for the job and even less for negotiating the web of bureaucratic rivalries into which it cast him. Within a few months he resigned and set up as a full-time novelist.

When Fontane told his publisher at the end of his sixth

decade that everything lay ahead of him he was right in one sense: at an age when most people look forward to retirement he embarked on twenty years of unremitting labour. Sitting at his desk in the small flat at 134c Potsdamer Strasse which he occupied from 1872, he wrote seventeen works of fiction and two volumes of memoirs, each manuscript given a fair copy by the long-suffering Emilie. But in another sense his remark is misleading, for while the novel proved to be the perfect conduit for his creative energies, his earlier efforts as a poet, journalist, critic, travel writer, historian and translator were not just a series of false starts. Together with a lifelong epistolary habit (and he is one of the best letter-writers in German), they honed his style and cultivated the feeling for character and anecdote that was first kindled by his father's 'Socratic method'.

He produced two historical novels, including his maiden work *Vor dem Sturm* (*Before the Storm*) of 1878, set in Prussia during the Napoleonic Wars; a few less convincing tales mixing suspense, crime and fate according to a then-fashionable formula; *Graf Petöfy* (*Count Petöfy*) of 1884, which portrays the perilous intimacy between the Viennese nobility and the world of the theatre; and *Unwiederbringlich* (*No Way Back*) of 1891, an elegiac story of squandered happiness set in Schleswig and Copenhagen and one of his most flawless works.[2] He is, though, most celebrated for his narratives of contemporary Berlin life. *L'Adultera* (*The Adulteress*) and *Cécile*, published in 1882 and 1887, depict the entrapment felt by women whose much older husbands deny them meaningful autonomy. *Irrungen, Wirrungen* (*Aberrations, Confusions*; translated here as *On Tangled Paths*) appeared in 1888, the thematically similar *Stine* in 1890, and *Frau Jenny Treibel*, a comedy of manners set among the wealthy bourgeoisie, in 1892.

But it was not until 1895 and *Effi Briest*, the story of a girl married by her parents to an apparently suitable but in fact most unsuitable man, that Fontane enjoyed his first major commercial success. This was followed in 1896 by *Die Poggenpuhls* (*The Poggenpuhls*), a critical but affectionate portrait of an aristocratic family fallen on hard times, and in 1898 by *Der Stechlin* (*Stechlin*), which suffuses the interwoven stories of two families with the author's philosophy of gradualism, engaged scepticism, and tolerance. The unfinished *Mathilde Möhring*, a richly comic narrative of an ambitious young woman carving out a career for her pliable but lazy husband, was written earlier but first published in 1907, nine years after Fontane's death at the age of seventy-eight on 20 September 1898.

These novels (several of which are short enough to be called novellas) depart from two dominant traditions in German fiction: the *Bildungsroman*, or novel of formation, which charts the shaping of a single person's identity from adolescence to adulthood through conflicts and accommodations with the world in which he lives; and Poetic Realism, the highly crafted tales set in provincial, sometimes idyllic and at any rate fairly static communities in which moral dilemmas can be presented free of larger social or political questions. Fontane's place is rather in the mainstream European school of social realism, with its close description of material reality, multiple characters embedded in complex social networks, and a rejection of the idealist, supernatural and escapist tendencies associated with Romanticism in favour of a more rationalistic world view.

On Tangled Paths clearly lies in this 'European' tradition. The newspaper serialization that preceded the book edition bore the subtitle 'An Everyday Berlin Story', and, while there is no known factual source, the tale of an affair between a seamstress and a lieutenant in an aristocratic regiment is really too straightforward to require one. In an odd compliment to the novel's verisimilitude, Fontane received a visit shortly after its appearance from a distressed woman in her mid-forties who claimed she was the seamstress and he had written her story. 'It was,' he recalled, 'a terrible scene with no end of wailing.'[3]

The novel is perhaps most obviously realistic in its attention to locale. During the writing process, which lasted with long interruptions from 1882 to 1887, Fontane visited important scenes and landmarks in the narrative like the Hinckeldey memorial on the Jungfern Heath, the Rollkrug Tavern, the New St James' Cemetery, and Hankel's Stowage. Topographical precision is established in the very first sentence, which pinpoints the Dörrs' market garden (which really existed, though the Dörrs themselves did not), and thereafter we are taken along real streets, past real buildings, and into real restaurants and shops. Fontane hoped his readers would enjoy 'the Berlin flavour of the thing',[4] and so lovingly is the city brought to life that it almost qualifies as a character in the narrative.

Equally precise is the time-frame. The story opens during the week after Whitsun 1875, Baron Botho von Rienäcker and Lene Nimptsch having become acquainted the preceding Easter Monday. They part at the beginning of July, and Botho marries his wealthy cousin Käthe von Sellenthin in September. Events of the next few months are briefly sketched in before the story is taken up again in May 1878. The novel ends with Lene's wedding in early August of that year.

Because *On Tangled Paths* describes scenes in the mid-seventies from the perspective of the mid-eighties, it is, in some degree, a document of change. The wording of the opening sentence makes it plain that the market garden no longer exists, and Berlin readers would have known it had succumbed to urban sprawl, just as the inn at Hankel's Stowage had been replaced by a colony of villas. This was the period of rapid industrialization and economic growth known as the *Gründerjahre* (Age of the Founders), and Berlin, from

1871 the capital of the new Reich, experienced a building boom that gave it the extent and grandeur of an imperial metropolis. Its population swelled too as migrants from rural areas arrived to take jobs in factories and on construction sites.

These changes naturally unsettled the aristocracy, whose agrarian wealth was now eclipsed by the fortunes of industrialists and financiers. However, blue blood still dominated the higher reaches of the army, politics, diplomacy, and the civil service, and had received a powerful fillip from Prussia's military successes. Titled officers in prestigious regiments were society's idols, a reality captured in chapter 6 when the thirteen-year-old porter's daughter looks up adoringly as Botho emerges from his flat in walking-out dress. Despite this glamour the lives of such men in peacetime often felt a little purposeless and, like the young officers we meet in chapter 8, they filled their time with cards, gossip, horses and mistresses. Meanwhile Botho's uncle Baron Osten represents the preceding generation of the nobility that held to the old Prussian values of unswerving honour, plain speaking and plain dealing and looked upon the clever but duplicitous Bismarck and his flashy new empire with distaste.

The other main group depicted in the novel is the working class, to which belong the Dörrs, the Nimptsches, and various minor figures, many with a distinctive Berlin twist: a cab driver, a shop assistant, a postman, a cemetery attendant, and several domestic servants. The general impression they create is of a capacity for hard work, a generous but unsentimental outlook, a caustic sense of humour, and an appetite for life's simple pleasures. All belong to the established lower orders rather than the new industrial masses, but nonetheless lead tough, precarious lives. Lene supports herself with piecework for one of the better textile firms, but her primitive living conditions and the physical decay of her foster-mother, ground down by an equally toilsome life, point to the vulnerability of her situation. Indeed, seamstresses, laundresses, milliners and shop girls often earned so little that they were obliged to accept a 'protector' from a higher station in life, a situation familiar from the representation of Parisian *grisettes* in literature and opera but equally prevalent in Berlin and personified here by the officers' companions introduced in chapter 13.

Lene has no resort to such expedients, and does not, it seems, benefit from her connection with Botho even to the extent of receiving gifts from him. Their relationship is based purely on mutual inclination, and it is Lene's pride to be her lover's equal in human terms. For his part, Botho displays occasional touches of condescension that are almost inevitable given the social and educational gulf between them, but always treats her with respect and delicacy. Deeply in love, they also understand that by temperament, taste and values they are perfectly matched. But a permanent union is out of the question, for while marriages of impecunious noblemen to daughters of the new plutocracy are by now too common to excite notice, marriage to such as Lene would mean Botho's banishment from his family and social circle, the forfeiture of his inheritance, and, most probably, the obligation to resign his commission.

It is easy to read a novel in which the social hierarchy bulks so large as politically motivated. The Marxist critic Georg Lukács believed it showed 'the moral, humanist superiority of the plebeian figures over the ruling class' and called Lene 'a triumph of the popular-plebeian'.[5] Such trenchancy is, however, unwarranted. For one thing, taking all the characters together, it is not true that virtue resides only at the bottom of the social scale and vice only at the top; for another, these characters are more than just products of their environment (Lene's lack of a Berlin accent underlines this). Although he wrote at a time when the Naturalist School, inspired by Zola, was in the ascendant in Germany, Fontane rejected its deterministic view of human beings as victims of poverty and hereditary flaws, as well as the political message that accompanies this 'scientific' approach.

This is not to say that Fontane is indifferent to social problems, simply that his critique is descriptive rather than reformatory, and that his main focus is on individual human subjects. Rather than the struggle of one class against another, or of a free-spirited person against external social constraints, *On Tangled Paths* examines the tension within that person's mind between social conditioning and the instinct for self-definition. In this way the theme of a cavalry officer's impossible love for a poor seamstress, itself of purely historical interest, gains universality as an exploration of the rival claims of self and society, integrity and accommodation that will always be with us. It is easy to censure past injustices, but any community at any time imposes 'dominant discourses' and behavioural norms on its members, who must overcome a part of what has become their own identity before they can go against the grain.

The lovers apprehend that the social obstacles to their happiness, while real and powerful, embody no eternal or essential human distinctions: Botho lacks the sense of class entitlement exhibited by his uncle and mother and is able to mock the vapidity of aristocratic life; and Lene differs from the other inhabitants of the market garden in viewing 'fine gentlemen' as people in better circumstances rather than beings apart. And yet neither of them rebels. She appears positively fixated by the thought that their relationship must end (though her remarks to this effect may enclose a forlorn hope that he will contradict her), while he interprets various 'messages' in his environment as warnings against breaking with caste and custom (though his rather tortured logic suggests an attempt to rationalize faintness of heart as devotion to order). Their refusal to entertain the possibility of marriage or even the settled concubinage that Botho's friend

Rexin plans with his mistress almost seems to make them advocates of the system that frustrates them.

And yet, are they wrong to give each other up so meekly? Botho's life after he leaves Lene is emotionally bleak, ever more so as the extent of his loss dawns on him, but staying faithful to her would have placed him in circumstances for which he is ill-adapted. This prospect, which he later conjures up as an admonition to Rexin, would mean the souring of their happiness and, for him, a probable loss of self-respect. Are they not, then, better off remaining in familiar circles with spouses who, for all their shortcomings, are both suitable and tolerable? In lesser hands this would be a story of 'good' individuals brought low by 'evil' society, and Gideon Franke and Käthe von Sellenthin would be ogres. But Fontane sees the necessity of a social order for the regulation of human affairs, even as he knows that the principles of the one he inhabits are transient and often unfair. Indeed he is as sceptical as his unheroic hero about defying the collective and seeking happiness in romantic isolation: partly because he believes man is a gregarious animal, and partly because he rejects the idea of a core of personality free from environmental conditioning.

These are some of the main lines of a sociological reading of the novel. Of course there have been many other approaches: feminists have analysed gender roles, comparatists have identified influences and parallels, and historical critics have explained political, economic and other contexts. There have been investigations into the uses of memory and imagination, of poetically charged settings, and of allusions to major literary texts and the stale formulas of popular fiction. Close readings have shed light on the structure and rhythms of Fontane's prose, while studies of individual characters have offered divergent evaluations of Frau Dörr, Käthe and Botho.

In a recent article I argue that Botho and Lene's determination to see their love bond as unique is undermined

by other characters, who reintegrate it into banal, impov-
erishing categories even before larger social forces compel
its dissolution. This process can be intentional, as when the
officers, irritated by Botho's belief that his love is 'special',
seek to reduce it to the recognizable template of an officer's
premarital affair with a working-class girl; or unintentional,
as when Frau Nimptsch treats the couple as typical lovebirds
or Frau Dörr regales them with saucy language that cheapens
their experience. Moreover, Botho himself never fully casts
off the clichéd patterns of thought and speech of his peers,
and while he claims to cherish Lene because she is 'different'
from others, his initial attraction is based on seeing her as an
artless, unspoilt girl living in an Arcadian setting – the biggest
cliché of all.[6]

Other interpreters have gone in search of 'the thousand
finesses' Fontane said he had woven into the text but feared
no one would perceive.[7] These include networks of verbal
motifs, in particular 'order', 'happiness' and 'binding', as
well as symbols like flowers/wreaths (representing love,
marriage and death) and Frau Nimptsch's fire (embodying
hospitality, comfort, and the reassuring continuity of life).
Tautly arranged patterns of anticipation and retrospection,
of parallel, echo and contrast, illuminate individual choices
and destinies. Thus Botho's inability to stand by Lene is
foreshadowed by Dörr's ornamental cock being put to flight
by the neighbour's dog in chapter 2, and his mockery of
aristocratic chatterboxes in chapter 4 acquires an irony at
his expense when he ends up marrying one. Certain recur-
rences set authenticity off against inauthenticity: a moonlight walk can be an unforgettable moment of delicate bliss
or a commonplace of romantic dalliance, and a woman
proffering a strawberry from her lips can be a spontaneous
gift of love or a routinized technique of allurement. Such
patterns are economical in their means, as are the repre-
sentative episodes – Botho's evening with the Nimptsches and

Dörrs, his lunch with his uncle, the officers bantering in their club – that distil countless similar exchanges.[8]

Fontane is an acknowledged master of dialogue, and this novel shows as well as any his skill in deploying myriad registers without trying his readers' patience by transcribing every dialectal tic or the fumblings and stutterings of real speech. As well as creating a vivid texture, dialogue plays a central role in character-drawing, which is effected not by introductory thumbnail sketches but by speakers revealing themselves in language and talking about one another – a technique that also enacts the theme of the struggle to maintain autonomous identity in the face of categorization by others. Meanwhile the narrator remains detached, often refusing to speculate about motivation, declaring ignorance on some matters and keeping discreetly silent about others. There are scenes of great poignancy, such as the lovers' final parting or the death of Frau Nimptsch, but their presentation is delicate and restrained, yielding an atmosphere of sorrow devoid of sentimentality. The implicit stance of the author is one of urbanity, gentle irony, and humanity – essentially the style of a sage old man.

Fontane's fear that readers would be oblivious of his craftsmanship was realized when the novel was printed in instalments by the *Vossische Zeitung* in July and August 1887. However, it was not the summer heat that impeded their appreciation, as he had predicted, but the scandalous content. The practice of well-situated bachelors having affairs with lower-class girls, though exceedingly common, was not discussed in the public sphere, and by depicting it without clear moral disapproval – indeed letting the lovers spend the night together as if this were perfectly normal – the author whipped up strong gusts of Victorian prudishness. Subscriptions to the newspaper were cancelled, and one of its owners wrote angrily to the chief editor, 'Won't this dreadful whore's tale soon be over?'[9]

Taken aback by this ferocity, Fontane prepared the ground carefully for the book publication by F. W. Steffens of Leipzig in January-February 1888. Well-disposed reviewers were alerted in advance, and no copies sent to the probably hostile conservative papers. The result was gratifying: a series of lengthy, serious-minded reviews praising his courage in tackling such a knotty theme, his evocative use of local colour, his skill at letting characters speak for themselves, and the winsomeness of his principals. The passage of time has only strengthened this esteem, while the initial objections soon lost their force. By 1910 the book was in its fifteenth edition, and according to the *Frankfurter Zeitung* in 1925 it was Fontane's best-selling title. Since the 1960s his status as the most important German novelist between Goethe and Thomas Mann has been firmly established, and this work is generally held to be among his three or four finest. It has been filmed twice, and is a common set text in German schools.

In English-speaking countries Fontane continues to be neglected outside the German departments of universities, despite the fact that as a social realist he wrote in a mainstream European rather than specifically German tradition.[10] Nonetheless the present work has already been translated four times: as *Trials and Tribulations* by Katherine Royce (1917); as *A Suitable Match* by Sandra Morris (1968); as *Entanglements* by Derek Bowman (1986), and as *Delusions, Confusions* by William L. Zwiebel (1989). I can only justify adding to this list by stating my belief that these versions fall too far short of the original in too many ways to allow readers to form a true idea of its quality. The present translation aims to convey as much as possible of the verve of dialogue and the fluent cadences, relaxed poise and wry humour of the descriptive and narrative passages—in other words what Thomas Mann, who was deeply influenced by it, called the 'Fontane tone'.

1. Letter of 18 August 1879 to Wilhelm Hertz (all letters cited here are in the edition of Fontane's works edited by Walter Keitel and Helmuth Nürnberger and published in Munich by Hanser, 1962-94).

2. Dates indicate first publication in book form, not prior appearance in newspaper or magazine instalments.

3. Letter of 20 September 1887 to Paul Schlenther.

4. Letter of 14 July 1887 to Emil Dominik ('flavour' in English in the original).

5. Georg Lukács, *German Realists in the Nineteenth Century*, translated by Jeremy Gaines and Paul Keast (Cambridge, MA: MIT Press, 1993), pages 326-27, 329.

6. Peter James Bowman, 'The Lover's Discourse in Theodor Fontane's *Irrungen, Wirrungen*', *Orbis Litterarum*, 62 (2007), pages 139-58.

7. Letter of 14 July 1887 to Emil Dominik.

8. For a full account of the novel's craftsmanship see the chapter-length study by M. A. McHaffie, 'Fontane's *Irrungen, Wirrungen* and the novel of Realism', in *Periods in German Literature*, volume II, edited by J. M. Ritchie (London: Wolff, 1969), pages 167-89.

9. Quoted on his own authority by Conrad Wandrey, *Theodor Fontane* (Munich: Beck, 1919), page 213.

10. For an excellent study of the reception of Fontane in the Anglophone world see Helen Chambers, *The Changing Image of Theodor Fontane* (Columbia, SC: Camden House, 1997), pages 97-130.

P. J. B.

Historical Persons and Places
Mentioned in *On Tangled Paths*

Achenbach. Andreas Achenbach (1815-1910) painted realistic but often dramatic German landscapes and seascapes. His brother Oswald (1827-1905), whose work Botho admires in chapter 7, specialized in colourful, warmly illuminated Italian views.

Arnim. Count Harry von Arnim-Suckow (1824-81), the German ambassador in Paris, was recalled by Bismarck in 1874 after opposing his decision to turn defeated France into a republic. His efforts to vindicate himself publicly using embassy documents led to an indictment for abuse of state papers. Arnim fled abroad and pursued a vendetta against Bismarck in the press, leading to a conviction in absentia for treason. Those who felt that Prussia owed its greatness to its leading families were outraged that a man of Arnim's caste should be pursued by state machinery in this way.

Bellevuestrasse. Elegant, tree-lined street located between the Potsdamer Platz and the southern limit of the Tiergarten.

Boitzenburg-Arnim. Count Friedrich Adolf von Arnim-Boitzenburg (1832-87), governor of Silesia, who resigned this post in protest at his brother-in-law Harry von Arnim's treatment by Bismarck. In 1880-81 he served as president of the Reichstag.

Borchardt's. Fashionable restaurant in the Französische Strasse.

Crown Prince. Prince Frederick of Prussia (1831-88), who as Frederick III was German Emperor for ninety-nine days in 1888. In 1858 he married Victoria (Vicky), Princess Royal of Great Britain and Ireland and daughter of Queen Victoria.

Dobeneck. Baron Ferdinand von Dobeneck (1791-1867), lieutenant-general in the Prussian army. He had fought against France in the Wars of Liberation of 1813-14.

Flora. Botanically themed café offering concerts and other entertainments.

Hankel's Stowage. In German *Hankels Ablage*, a landing-place and retreat for Berliners on the west bank of Lake Zeuthen, located to the south-east of the city and fed by the River Dahme. Fontane stayed and wrote eight chapters of the novel there in May 1884.

Heidelberg Barrel. Celebrated huge vat in the cellar of Heidelberg Castle, built in 1751 with a capacity of over 220,000 litres.

Hertel. Albert Hertel (1843-1912) was primarily a landscapist, but also painted still-lifes and genre scenes.

Hiller's. Fashionable restaurant in Unter den Linden.

Humboldt. Alexander von Humboldt (1769-1859), a naturalist and explorer who advanced the disciplines of botany and geography. His best-known work, an account of a five-year expedition to Central and South America, filled thirty-five volumes.

Kroll Gardens. Outdoor restaurant with musical entertainment in the Tiergarten.

Landgrafenstrasse. Aristocratic residential street in the Tiergarten.

Manteuffel. Field Marshal Baron Edwin von Manteuffel (1809-85), who as chief of the military cabinet from 1857 played a major role in reorganizing the Prussian army.

Moltke. Field Marshal Count Helmuth von Moltke (1800-91), chief of the Prussian General Staff from 1857. His modernization of the army was central to the victories against Denmark in 1864, Austria in 1866, and France in 1870-71.

Neumark. Literally 'New March', a region of Brandenburg lying east of the River Oder mainly given over to forestry and agriculture.

Ranke. Leopold von Ranke (1795-1886), the leading figure in the nineteenth-century German school of objective historians. His collected works (1867-90) ran to fifty-four volumes.

Renz's. Circus established by Ernst Jakob Renz in 1846.

Rollkrug. Famous tavern, pulled down in 1907, on the road descending into Berlin from the Teltow plateau south of the city.

Rollen means 'to roll' and *Krug* is Low German for 'inn', the idea being that vehicles could roll down to or from the building.

Saxon Switzerland. Area of forested sandstone hills near Dresden famous for its medieval fortresses, including Königstein, and its striking rock formations, including the Bastei (bastion).

Schlangenbad. Spa resort in the Taunus mountains, not far from Wiesbaden. In the nineteenth century its thermal springs were prescribed for gynaecological disorders. Bad Schwalbach, another watering place, lies just to the north.

Sibylline Books. Prophecies purchased from a sibyl, or prophetess, by Tarquinius Superbus, the last king of Rome. According to legend she offered him nine volumes of prophecies, but he refused her price. She then burnt three and offered him the other six for the same sum. When he again refused she burnt three more. To save the remaining volumes from destruction the king bought them for the original price.

Sorbian. The Sorbs, or Wends, are a Slavic population settled in Brandenburg and Saxony since the sixth century. Once a large population, they now number about 50,000.

Spandau. Industrial and garrison town to the south-east of Berlin, now part of the city.

Stralau. Village picturesquely situated on a tongue of land between the River Spree and Rummelsburg Lake to the south-east (in the nineteenth century) of Berlin.

Tiergarten. Literally 'Animal Garden', this former royal hunting estate was laid out as a park in the 1830s, but included public and commercial buildings as well as superior residential streets. Now the area is at the heart of the capital's political and financial district.

Tübbecke's. Tavern in Stralau run by the Tübbecke family for most of the nineteenth century.

Wilmersdorf. Village south-west of Berlin, now in the Charlottenburg–Wilmersdorf district of the city.

Zoological Gardens. Opened in 1844 with animals donated from the private menagerie of Frederick William IV of Prussia.